EVERY DAY
IS TO-DAY

GERTRUDE STEIN

EVERY DAY
IS TO-DAY

Essential Writings

Selected and Introduced
by Francesca Wade

PUSHKIN PRESS
LONDON

Pushkin Press
Somerset House, Strand
London WC2R 1LA

Introduction © Francesca Wade 2023

First published by Pushkin Press in 2023

1 3 5 7 9 8 6 4 2

ISBN 13: 978-1-78227-879-5

Permission to reproduce the following stories granted by the Estate of
Gertrude Stein / David Higham Associates: 'Flirting at the Bon Marche'
'Susie Asado', 'Cezanne', 'Van or Twenty Years Later', 'Identify a Poem',
'What Does She See When She Shuts Her Eyes', 'A Waterfall and Piano'

Frontispiece © Everett Collection Historical / Alamy Stock Photo

Designed and typeset by Tetragon, London

Printed and bound in Great Britain by TJ Books Limited,
Padstow, Cornwall on Munken Premium White 80gsm

www.pushkinpress.com

CONTENTS

INTRODUCTION

One autumn day in 1934, two women, recently arrived from Paris, entered a grocery store in central Manhattan. The owner glanced up and greeted them without missing a beat. 'How do you do, Miss Stein,' he said casually, as if he'd been expecting her. 'It must be pleasant coming back after thirty years.' As the women passed on through Times Square, squinting up at the billboards advertising Chevrolet, Wrigley's and Coca-Cola, one nudged the other and they looked up, together, at the tickertape snaking around the New York Times building, flashing breaking news to all who passed beneath. 'Gertrude Stein has arrived,' it read in electric lights.

'One of the most talked-about authors in the world returns to America this week,' read a report in *Newsweek*. 'Some people call her the "most intelligent American woman alive today"; others say she is crazy.' Stein's tour had been organised to promote her bestselling memoir, *The Autobiography of Alice B. Toklas* (1933), which she had written over six weeks the previous summer, hoping to earn the fame and readership which—at age 59—she feared was passing her by. Its story is, by now, one of legend: of her arrival in Paris from America in 1903; her immersion in the city's artistic world as the eccentric host of Saturday evening salons attended by writers and artists from Guillaume Apollinaire to Pablo Picasso, Henri Matisse to Ernest Hemingway, Juan Gris to F. Scott Fitzgerald; and her self-proclaimed 'genius' as a radical innovator who set out, in her life and work, to 'kill the nineteenth century'. The autobiography—an audacious act of knowing artifice, employing the voice of her long-term partner to portray Stein as she wanted to be seen—was an instant sensation. Its publication cata-pulted Stein to international celebrity—yet threatened to submerge her in the very fictions she had created.

Stein had written the book with an ulterior motive. She was fed up with decades of mockery and poor sales for the avant-garde texts she considered her 'real' writ-ing—her 1,000-page epic novel *The Making of Americans*, printed in 1925 by a now-defunct Parisian press; the books she and Toklas had self-financed through their own press, the Plain Edition, including her pastoral romance *Lucy Church Amiably* and *How to Write*, a series of meditations on sentences, narrative and grammar; the hundreds of short portraits, plays and poems published long ago in small magazines or languishing, unread, in filing cabinets—and hoped the autobiography would win her a new generation of readers willing to take her writing seriously. But, ironically, the book's huge success cemented the public image of Stein as a personality; a collector of other talents, rather than an artist in her own right. Up to this point, Stein had hesitated to explain her work, insisting that 'compositions are complete only if they are self-explanatory, requiring no interpretations beyond what they are.' But when Stein was invited to undertake a lecture tour of America, she saw the opportunity to elucidate her method in person. This was, she decided, a chance for doubting readers to learn how to read Stein from Stein herself; to turn attention away from the gossipy *Autobiography* and back to her older, notoriously 'difficult' work, and make the case for its importance—and, crucially, for its pleasure. 'If you understand a thing you enjoy it,' she told a bemused reporter, 'and if you enjoy a thing you understand it.' Over the course of six lectures, repeated in packed halls at universities, clubs and galleries in thirty-seven cities, she set out to challenge prevailing assumptions and convince readers that her work required no prior knowledge or intellectual framework; that there was no secret code to be deciphered, no key to the riddle. All that was needed, she repeated, was an open mind.

Throughout Stein's writing life, she had been preoccupied with questions of identity and perception: what it might mean to truly see another person or object, and to express their essence in language. As a medical student at the dawn of the twentieth century, reading her way through English literature in her spare time, Stein became fascinated by the inner workings of personality, and curious to isolate the forces that differentiated people from one another, and made each individual themselves. Around 1911, as Stein explained in her lecture 'Portraits and Repetition', she set aside her novel *The Making of Americans*, in which she set out to write 'a complete history of everyone', drawing on years of close study of friends, acquaintances and strangers, and began work on a series of short compositions which she called 'portraits'. Taking their cues from people she knew, often the artists who attended her Saturday evenings – Matisse, Picasso, Gris – Stein's word-portraits are radical experiments in conveying character without any narrative or straightforward description. Stein believed the way to understand others was not by what they said or did but by discovering what she described as their 'bottom nature': 'what is moving inside them that makes them them'. Her sustained use of repetition—which led one medical journalist to diagnose her with a rare form of echolalia—derived from her conviction that personality reveals itself through the 'infinite variations' in the way people repeat their characteristic gestures and phrases over time.

'The business of art,' Stein insisted, 'is to live in the actual present, that is the complete actual present, and to completely express that complete actual present.' Stein wanted her work to convey a sense of ongoing motion, a shifting dynamic, that would unfold on the page as if in real time. In her texts, Stein set out to strip language of its prior associations so that her words would mean something fresh and specific, unique to the particular context she was giving them. Seeking to counter the falsity she had begun to associate with purely representational art, Stein wanted her writing to feel not like a description of a thing, but the 'thing in itself': not imitation, but 'intellectual recreation.' If a text is to feel truly alive, she argued, it must exist not only in relation to something separate from it – the thing or person it's representing – but it 'must have its own life'. Trying to describe things so an imagined audience might recognise them, she believed, created distance rather than immediacy: if you're focused on creating a replica, you aren't really seeing beyond the surface, or creating in the moment. In Stein's work, words follow others not to advance a story, but to move the piece forward through associative logic, verbal echo, or pure insistence. At the University of Chicago, in response to a student's question about her famous and much-parodied line 'rose is a rose is a rose' (which first appeared in her 1913 text 'Sacred Emily'), Stein summed up her approach: 'You all have seen hundreds of poems about roses and you know in your bones that the rose is not there. I'm no fool; but I think that in that line the rose is red for the first time in English poetry for a hundred years.'

Stein's work defies traditional ways of reading. It's impossible, for one thing, to say what her texts are about. Even though they often start from concrete source material—objects in Stein's sightline, snippets of conversation, the people around her—they aren't so much *about* that ostensible subject-matter, but engage with the way the words work together on the page, re-forming everyday experience in surreal mutations of language. Reading Stein can feel like a slow-motion experience of perception dawning. Often, a noun or phrase establishes itself through repetition, tests its strength with slight variations, before puns and jokes and ambiguities flood in as the words themselves take over, emerging with a momentum all their own. Stein called her process of writing 'meditation', and reading her work feels as close as possible to experiencing its composition in real time, as Stein focuses in on an image, swaps a syllable for a homophone, prods at words and makes them fizz. Writing, for Stein, came out of deep concentration, and her work lays bare both the struggle of its creation and the triumph of finding the next idea. 'I am I not any longer when I see,' wrote Stein: in shedding words' associations and referents, Stein was also shaking herself out of the text, attempting to forget her audience and write as un-self-consciously as possible. She wanted to break every habit, never to fall back on cliches or formulas that she considered numbing to active thought. Her work is a celebration of chaos and mutability, a rejoinder to rules, where words are set free from the shackles of meaning and grammatical function, made unfamiliar, and charged with power to make the world afresh. Her untiring quest for alternative ways of thinking extended, in her life, to her longstanding interest in astrology, prophecy and the lives of saints; her rejection of hierarchy and convention in her writing mirrors her resolutely unpatriarchal household.

Stein left few clues to her work beyond her lectures: she didn't keep a diary, rarely discussed her writing in letters, and refused—despite many requests from admirers and detractors alike—to write introductions or explanations. From the notebooks, manuscripts and correspondence in Stein's enormous archive (held at Yale's Beinecke Library) it's possible to piece together fragments of context: to know, for example, that 'Idem the Same: A Valentine to Sherwood Anderson' was originally written for Toklas, but that Stein changed the title

in gratitude after Anderson wrote an introduction to her
1922 book *Geography and Plays*; that 'Miss Furr and Miss
Skeene'—now considered one of the earliest examples
of the word 'gay' used in its sexual context—was based
on Ethel Mars and Maud Squire, two artist friends of
Stein and Toklas; that 'Susie Asado' and 'Preciosilla'
are companion pieces inspired by the whirling skirts
of Spanish dancers; that 'Identity a Poem' was written
for a puppeteer she met on the streets of Chicago, who
asked her to compose something for his marionettes.
That 'Ladies' Voices' stemmed from eavesdropping on
a group of strangers in Mallorca, and recalls the plot-
less dinner-party conversation of 'What Happened',
Stein's first play; that plays, after portraits, became the
form in which Stein developed her idea of time as a
landscape, where events might occur not in linear order
but simultaneously.

Stein's attempts to find a wider audience for her
earlier work were not entirely successful. While a devoted
coterie of readers convinced of her importance sought
out and passed around dog-eared copies of Plain Edition
titles and *transition* magazine, publishers continued to
reject her new and old work, asking instead for more

charming anecdotes in the style of the *Autobiography*. At Stein's death, in July 1946, much of the work she considered her best remained out of print: some of the texts that follow were not published at all in her lifetime, while others have a material history central to Stein's literary legend. Mabel Dodge, Stein's first great promoter, bound copies of 'Portrait of Mabel Dodge at the Villa Curonia' in Florentine wallpaper and gave them to visitors at her Fifth Avenue soirees, while 'Matisse' and 'Picasso' were first published in Alfred Stieglitz's influential magazine *Camera Work*, and distributed at the 1913 Armory Show—the first, shocking display of their paintings in America—alongside an essay by Dodge describing Stein as 'the only woman in the world who has put the spirit of post-impressionism into prose'. From the archive, we can discern how her amused disregard for genre distinctions and her appetite for popular culture—including her abiding love of detective stories—manifest in 'A Waterfall and a Piano', 'A Movie' and 'Advertisements', while in 'Identity a Poem'—part of a wave of self-questioning texts written after the *Autobiography*—we meet an older Stein, meditating on the disconcerting effects of fame. The presiding context for all Stein's writing, of course, is her relationship with Alice B. Toklas. Stein's notebooks often began with dedications to Toklas, and their love is inscribed throughout this volume in double-entendres, songs and codes, from 'Ada', Stein's first portrait, a retelling of Toklas's own account of her life story, to 'A Book Concluding With As A Wife Has A Cow A Love Story', a second portrait of Toklas which intertwines the joy of sexuality and writing in a glorious explosion of eroticism.

'I like the feeling of words doing as they want to do and as they have to do,' Stein wrote. The texts that follow are founded on pleasure and sensuality, the thrill of making something new, the intimacy of really paying attention. Stein's bewitching work probes the possibilities of language more deeply than any writer before or since: her restless pursuit of things as they are creates a body of writing as alive as any work of art can be. More than a hundred years on, Stein's rose is as red is it ever was.

Francesca Wade

EVERY DAY
IS TO-DAY

ADA

Barnes Colhard did not say he would not do it but he did not do it. He did at it and then he did not do at it, he did not ever think about it. He just thought some time he might do something.

His father Mr. Abram Colhard spoke about it to every one and very many of them spoke to Barnes Colhard about it and he always listened to them.

Then Barnes fell in love with a very nice girl and she would not marry him. He cried then, his father Mr. Abram Colhard comforted him and they took a trip and Barnes promised he would do what his father wanted him to be doing. He did not do the thing, he thought he would do another thing, he did not do the other thing, his father Mr. Colhard did not want him to do the other thing. He really did not do anything then. When he was a good deal older he married a very rich girl. He had thought perhaps he would not propose to her but his sister wrote to him that it would be a good thing. He married the rich girl and she thought he was the most wonderful man and one who knew everything. Barnes never spent more than the income of the fortune he and his wife had then, that is to say they did not spend more than the income and this was a surprise to very many who knew about him and about his marrying the girl who had such a large fortune. He had a happy life while he was living and after he was dead his wife and children remembered him.

He had a sister who also was successful enough in being one being living. His sister was one who came to be happier than most people come to be in living. She came to be a completely happy one. She was twice as old as her brother. She had been a very good daughter to her mother. She and her mother had always told very pretty stories to each other. Many old men loved to hear her tell these stories to her mother. Every one who ever knew her mother liked her mother. Many were sorry later that not every one liked the daughter. Many did like the daughter but not every one as every one had liked the mother. The daughter was charming inside in her, it did not show outside in her to every one, it certainly did to some. She did sometimes think her mother would be pleased with a story that did not please her mother. When her mother later was sicker the daughter knew that there were some stories she could tell her that would not please her mother. Her mother died and really mostly altogether the mother and the daughter had told each other stories very happily together.

The daughter then kept house for her father and took care of her brother. There were many relations who lived with them. The daughter did not like them to live with them and she did not like them to die with them. The daughter, Ada they had called her after her grandmother who had delightful ways of smelling flowers and eating dates and sugar, did not like it at all then as she did not like so much dying and she did not like any of the living she was doing then. Every now and then some old gentlemen told delightful stories to her. Mostly then there were not nice stories told by any one then in her living. She told her father Mr. Abram Colhard that she did not like it at all being one being living then. He never said anything. She was afraid then, she was one needing charming stories and happy telling of them and not having that thing she was always trembling. Then every one who could live with them were dead and there were then the father and the son a young man then and the daughter coming to be that one then. Her grandfather had left some money to them each one of them. Ada said she was going to use it to go away from them. The father said nothing then, then he said something and she said nothing then, then they both said nothing and then it was that she went away from them. The father was quite tender then, she was his daughter then. He wrote her tender letters then, she wrote him tender letters then, she never went back to live with him. He wanted her to come and she wrote him tender letters then. He liked the tender letters she wrote to him. He wanted her to live with him. She answered him by writing tender letters to him and telling very nice stories indeed in them. He wrote nothing and then he wrote again and there was some waiting and then he wrote tender letters again and again.

She came to be happier than anybody else who was living then. It is easy to believe this thing. She was telling some one, who was loving every story that was charming. Some one who was living was almost always listening.

Some one who was loving was almost always listening. That one who was loving was almost always listening. That one who was loving was telling about being one then listening. That one being loving was then telling stories having a beginning and a middle and an ending. That one was then one always completely listening. Ada was then one and all her living then one completely telling stories that were charming, completely listening to stories having a beginning and a middle and an ending. Trembling was all living, living was all loving, some one was then the other one. Certainly this one was loving this Ada then. And certainly Ada all her living then was happier in living than any one else who ever could, who was, who is, who ever will be living.

1910

MATISSE

One was quite certain that for a long part of his being one being living he had been trying to be certain that he was wrong in doing what he was doing and then when he could not come to be certain that he had been wrong in doing what he had been doing, when he had completely convinced himself that he would not come to be certain that he had been wrong in doing what he had been doing he was really certain then that he was a great one and he certainly was a great one. Certainly every one could be certain of this thing that this one is a great one.

Some said of him, when anybody believed in him they did not then believe in any other one. Certainly some said this of him.

He certainly very clearly expressed something. Some said that he did not clearly express anything. Some were certain that he expressed something very clearly and some of such of them said that he would have been a greater one if he had not been one so clearly expressing what he was expressing. Some said he was not clearly expressing what he was expressing and some of such of them said that the greatness of struggling which was not clear expression made of him one being a completely great one.

Some said of him that he was greatly expressing something struggling. Some said of him that he was not greatly expressing something struggling.

He certainly was clearly expressing something, certainly sometime any one might come to know that of him. Very many did come to know it of him that he was clearly expressing what he was expressing. He was a great one. Any one might come to know that of him. Very many did come to know that of him. Some who came to know that of him, that he was a great one, that he was clearly expressing something, came then to be certain that he was not greatly expressing something being struggling. Certainly he was expressing something being struggling. Any one could be certain that he was expressing something being struggling. Some were certain that he was greatly expressing this thing. Some were certain that he was not greatly expressing this thing. Every one could come to be certain that he was a great man. Any one could come to be certain that he was clearly expressing something.

Some certainly were wanting to be needing to be doing what he was doing, that is clearly expressing something. Certainly they were willing to be wanting to be a great one. They were, that is some of them, were not wanting to be needing expressing anything being struggling. And certainly he was one not greatly express- ing something being struggling, he was a great one, he was clearly expressing something. Some were wanting to be doing what he was doing that is clearly expressing something. Very many were doing what he was doing, not greatly expressing something being struggling. Very many were wanting to be doing what he was doing were not wanting to be expressing anything being struggling.

There were very many wanting to be doing what he was doing that is to be one clearly expressing something. He was certainly a great man, any one could be really certain of this thing, every one could be certain of this thing. There were very many who were wanting to be ones doing what he was doing that is to be ones clearly expressing something and then very many of them were not wanting to be being ones doing that thing, that is clearly expressing something, they wanted to be ones expressing something being struggling, something being going to be some other thing, something being going to be something some one sometime would be clearly expressing and that would be something that would be a thing then that would then be greatly expressing some other thing than that thing, certainly very many were then not wanting to be doing what this one was doing clearly expressing something and some of them had been ones wanting to be doing that thing wanting to be ones clearly expressing something. Some were wanting to be ones doing what this one was doing wanted to be ones clearly expressing something. Some of such of them were ones certainly clearly expressing something, that was in them a thing not really interesting then any other one. Some of such of them went on being all their living ones wanting to be clearly expressing something and some of them were clearly expressing something.

This one was one very many were knowing some and very many were glad to meet him, very many sometimes

listened to him, some listened to him very often, there
were some who listened to him, and he talked then
and he told them then that certainly he had been one
suffering and he was then being one trying to be certain
that he was wrong in doing what he was doing and he
had come then to be certain that he never would be
certain that he was doing what it was wrong for him
to be doing then and he was suffering then and he was
certain that he would be one doing what he was doing
and he was certain that he should be one doing what he
was doing and he was certain that he would always be
one suffering and this then made him certain this, that
he would always be one being suffering, this made him
certain that he was expressing something being struggling and certainly very many were quite certain that he
was greatly expressing something being struggling. This
one was one knowing some who were listening to him
and he was telling very often about being one suffering
and this was not a dreary thing to any one hearing that
then, it was not a saddening thing to any one hearing it
again and again, to some it was quite an interesting thing
hearing it again and again, to some it was an exciting
thing hearing it again and again, some knowing this one

and being certain that this one was a great man and was one clearly expressing something were ones hearing this one telling about being one being living were hearing this one telling this thing again and again. Some who were ones knowing this one and were ones certain that this one was one who was clearly telling something, was a great man, were not listening very often to this one telling again and again about being one being living. Certainly some who were certain that this one was a great man and one clearly expressing something and greatly expressing something being struggling were listening to this one telling about being living telling about this again and again and again. Certainly very many knowing this one and being certain that this one was a great man and that this one was clearly telling something were not listening to this one telling about being living, were not listening to this one telling this again and again.

This one was certainly a great man, this one was certainly clearly expressing something. Some were certain that this one was clearly expressing something being struggling, some were certain that this one was not greatly expressing something being struggling.

Very many were not listening again and again to this one telling about being one being living. Some were listening again and again to this one telling about this one being one being in living.

Some were certainly wanting to be doing what this one was doing that is were wanting to be ones clearly expressing something. Some of such of them did not go on in being ones wanting to be doing what this one was doing that is in being ones clearly expressing something. Some went on being ones wanting to be doing what this one was doing that is, being ones clearly expressing something. Certainly this one was one who was a great man. Any one could be certain of this thing. Every one would come to be certain of this thing. This one was one certainly clearly expressing something. Any one could come to be certain of this thing. Every one would come to be certain of this thing. This one was one, some were quite certain, one greatly expressing something being struggling. This one was one, some were quite certain, one not greatly expressing something being struggling.

1911

PICASSO

One whom some were certainly following was one who was completely charming. One whom some were certainly following was one who was charming. One whom some were following was one who was completely charming. One whom some were following was one who was certainly completely charming.

Some were certainly following and were certain that the one they were then following was one working and was one bringing out of himself then something. Some were certainly following and were certain that the one they were then following was one bringing out of himself then something that was coming to be a heavy thing, a solid thing and a complete thing.

One whom some were certainly following was one working and certainly was one bringing something out of himself then and was one who had been all his living had been one having something coming out of him.

Something had been coming out of him, certainly it had been coming out of him, certainly it was something, certainly it had been coming out of him and it had meaning, a charming meaning, a solid meaning, a struggling meaning, a clear meaning.

One whom some were certainly following and some were certainly following him, one whom some were certainly following was one certainly working.

One whom some were certainly following was one having something coming out of him something having meaning and this one was certainly working then.

This one was working and something was coming then, something was coming out of this one then. This one was one and always there was something coming out of this one and always there had been something coming out of this one. This one had never been one not having something coming out of this one. This one was one having something coming out of this one. This one had been one whom some were following. This one was one whom some were following. This one was being one whom some were following. This one was one who was working.

34

This one was one who was working. This one was one being one having something being coming out of him. This one was one going on having something come out of him. This one was one going on working. This one was one whom some were following. This one was one who was working.

This one always had something being coming out of this one. This one was working. This one always had been working. This one was always having something that was coming out of this one that was a solid thing, a charming thing, a lovely thing, a perplexing thing, a disconcerting thing, a simple thing, a clear thing, a complicated thing, an interesting thing, a disturbing thing, a repellent thing, a very pretty thing. This one was one certainly being one having something coming out of him. This one was one whom some were following. This one was one who was working.

This one was one who was working and certainly this one was needing to be working so as to be one being working. This one was one having something coming out of him. This one would be one all his living having something coming out of him. This one was working and then this one was working and this one was needing to be working, not to be one having something coming out of him something having meaning, but was needing to be working so as to be one working.

This one was certainly working and working was something this one was certain this one would be doing and this one was doing that thing, this one was working. This one was not one completely working. This one was not ever completely working. This one certainly was not completely working.

This one was one having always something being coming out of him, something having completely a real meaning. This one was one whom some were following. This one was one who was working. This one was one who was working and he was one needing this thing needing to be working so as to be one having some way of being one having some way of working. This one was one who was working. This one was one having something come out of him something having meaning. This one was one always having something come out of him and this thing the thing coming out of him always had real meaning. This one was one who was working. This one was one who was almost always working. This one was not one completely working. This one was one not ever completely working. This one was not one working to have anything come out of him. This one did have something having meaning that did come out of him. He always did have something come out of him. He was working, he was not ever completely working. He did have some following. They were always following him. Some were certainly following him. He was one who was working. He was one having something coming out of him something having meaning. He was not ever completely working.

1911

MISS FURR AND MISS SKEENE

Helen Furr had quite a pleasant home. Mrs. Furr was quite a pleasant woman. Mr. Furr was quite a pleasant man. Helen Furr had quite a pleasant voice a voice quite worth cultivating. She did not mind working. She worked to cultivate her voice. She did not find it gay living in the same place where she had always been living. She went to a place where some were cultivating something, voices and other things needing cultivating. She met Georgine Skeene there who was cultivating her voice which some thought was quite a pleasant one. Helen Furr and Georgine Skeene lived together then. Georgine Skeene liked travelling. Helen Furr did not care about travelling, she liked to stay in one place and be gay there. They were together then and travelled to another place and stayed there and were gay there.

They stayed there and were gay there, not very gay there, just gay there. They were both gay there, they were regularly working there both of them cultivating their voices there, they were both gay there. Georgine Skeene was gay there and she was regular, regular in being gay, regular in not being gay, regular in being a gay one who was one not being gay longer than was needed to be one being quite a gay one. They were both gay then there and both working there then.

They were in a way both gay there where there were many cultivating something. They were both regular in being gay there. Helen Furr was gay there, she was gayer and gayer there and really she was just gay there, she was gayer and gayer there, that is to say she found ways of being gay there that she was using in being gay there. She was gay there, not gayer and gayer, just gay there, that is to say she was not gayer by using the things she found there that were gay things, she was gay there, always she was gay there.

They were quite regularly gay there, Helen Furr and Georgine Skeene, they were regularly gay there where they were gay. They were very regularly gay.

To be regularly gay was to do every day the gay

thing that they did every day. To be regularly gay was to end every day at the same time after they had been regularly gay. They were regularly gay. They were gay every day. They ended every day in the same way, at the same time, and they had been every day regularly gay.

The voice Helen Furr was cultivating was quite a pleasant one. The voice Georgine Skeene was cultivating was, some said, a better one. The voice Helen Furr was cultivating she cultivated and it was quite completely a pleasant enough one then, a cultivated enough one then. The voice Georgine Skeene was cultivating she did not cultivate too much. She cultivated it quite some. She cultivated and she would sometime go on cultivating it and it was not then an unpleasant one, it would not be then an unpleasant one, it would be a quite richly enough cultivated one, it would be quite richly enough to be a pleasant enough one.

They were gay where there were many cultivating something. The two were gay there, were regularly gay there. Georgine Skeene would have liked to do more travelling. They did some travelling, not very much travelling, Georgine Skeene would have liked to do more travelling, Helen Furr did not care about doing travelling, she liked to stay in a place and be gay there.

They stayed in a place and were gay there, both of them stayed there, they stayed together there, they were gay there, they were regularly gay there.

They went quite often, not very often, but they did go back to where Helen Furr had a pleasant enough home and then Georgine Skeene went to a place where her brother had quite some distinction. They both went, every few years, went visiting to where Helen Furr had quite a pleasant home. Certainly Helen Furr would not find it gay to stay, she did not find it gay, she said she would not stay, she said she did not find it gay, she said she would not stay where she did not find it gay, she said she found it gay where she did stay and she did stay there where very many were cultivating something. She did stay there. She always did find it gay there.

She went to see them where she had always been living and where she did not find it gay. She had a pleasant home there, Mrs. Furr was a pleasant enough woman, Mr. Furr was a pleasant enough man, Helen told them and they were not worrying, that she did not find it gay living where she had always been living.

Georgine Skeene and Helen Furr were living where they were both cultivating their voices and they were gay there. They visited where Helen Furr had come from and then they went to where they were living where they were then regularly living.

There were some dark and heavy men there then. There were some who were not so heavy and some who were not so dark. Helen Furr and Georgine Skeene sat regularly with them. They sat regularly with the ones who were dark and heavy. They sat regularly with the ones who were not so dark. They sat regularly with the ones that were not so heavy. They sat with them regularly, sat with some of them. They went with them regularly went with them. They were regular then, they were gay then, they were where they wanted to be then where it was gay to be then, they were regularly gay then. There were men there then who were dark and heavy and they sat with them with Helen Furr and Georgine Skeene and they went with them with Miss Furr and Miss Skeene, and they went with the heavy and dark men Miss Furr and Miss Skeene went with them, and they sat with them, Miss Furr and Miss Skeene sat with them, and there were other men, some were not heavy men and they sat with Miss Furr and Miss Skeene and Miss Furr and Miss Skeene sat with them, and there were other men who were not dark men and they sat with Miss Furr and Miss Skeene and Miss Furr and Miss Skeene sat with them. Miss Furr and Miss Skeene went with them and they went with Miss Furr and Miss Skeene, some who were not heavy men, some who were not dark men. Miss Furr and Miss Skeene sat regularly, they sat with some men. Miss Furr and Miss Skeene went and there were some men with them. There were men and Miss Furr and Miss Skeene went with them, went somewhere with them, went with some of them.

Helen Furr and Georgine Skeene were regularly living where very many were living and cultivating in themselves something. Helen Furr and Georgine Skeene were living very regularly then, being very regular then in being gay then. They did then learn many ways to be gay and they were then being gay being quite regular in being gay, being gay and they were learning little things, little things in ways of being gay, they were very regular then, they were learning very many little things in ways of being gay, they were being gay and using these little things they were learning to have to be gay with

43

regularly gay with then, and they were gay the same amount they had been gay. They were quite gay, they were quite regular, they were learning little things, gay little things, they were gay inside them the same amount they had been gay, they were gay the same length of time they had been gay every day.

They were regular in being gay, they learned little things that are things in being gay, they learned many little things that are things in being gay, they were gay every day, they were regular, they were gay, they were gay the same length of time every day, they were gay, they were quite regularly gay.

Georgine Skeene went away to stay two months with her brother. Helen Furr did not go then to stay with her father and her mother. Helen Furr stayed there where they had been regularly living the two of them and she would then certainly not be lonesome, she would go on being gay. She did go on being gay. She was not any more gay but she was gay longer every day than they had been being gay when they were together being gay. She was gay then quite exactly the same way. She learned a few more little ways of being in being gay. She was quite gay and in the same way, the same way she had been gay and she was gay a little longer in the day, more of each day she was gay. She was gay longer every day than when the two of them had been being gay. She was gay quite in the way they had been gay, quite in the same way.

She was not lonesome then, she was not at all feeling any need of having Georgine Skeene. She was not astonished at this thing. She would have been a little astonished by this thing but she knew she was not astonished at anything and so she was not astonished at this thing not astonished at not feeling any need of having Georgine Skeene.

Helen Furr had quite a completely pleasant voice and it was quite well enough cultivated and she could use it and she did use it but then there was not any way of working at cultivating a completely pleasant voice when it has become a quite completely well enough cultivated one, and there was not much use in using it when one was not wanting it to be helping to make one a gay one. Helen Furr was not needing using her voice to be a gay one. She was gay then and sometimes she used her voice and she was not using it very often. It was quite completely enough cultivated and it was quite completely a pleasant one and she did not use it very often. She was then, she was quite exactly as gay as she had been, she was gay a little longer in the day than she had been.

She was gay exactly the same way. She was never tired of being gay that way. She had learned very many little ways to use in being gay. Very many were telling about using other ways in being gay. She was gay enough, she was always gay exactly the same way, she was always learning little things to use in being gay, she was telling about using other ways in being gay, she was telling about learning other ways in being gay, she was learning other ways in being gay, she would be using other ways in being gay, she would always be gay in the same way, when Georgine Skeene was there not so long each day as when Georgine Skeene was away.

She came to using many ways in being gay, she came to use every way in being gay. She went on living where many were cultivating something and she was gay, she had used every way to be gay.

They did not live together then Helen Furr and Georgine Skeene. Helen Furr lived there the longer where they had been living regularly together. Then neither of them were living there any longer. Helen Furr was living somewhere else then and telling some about being gay and she was gay then and she was living quite regularly then. She was regularly gay then. She was quite regular in being gay then. She remembered all the little ways of being gay. She used all the little ways of being gay. She was quite regularly gay. She told many then the way of being gay, she taught very many then little ways they could use in being gay. She was living very well, she was gay then, she went on living then, she was regular in being gay, she always was living very well and was gay very well and was telling about little ways one could be learning to use in being gay, and later was telling them quite often, telling them again and again.

1911

FLIRTING AT THE
BON MARCHE

Some know very well that their way of living is a sad one. Some know that their way of living is a dreary thing. Some know very well that their way of being living is a tedious one. Some know very well that they are living in a very dull way of living. Some do not know that a way of living is a tedious one. Some do not know that a way of living is a sad one. Some do not know that a way of living is a dreary way of living. Some do not know that one way of living is a dull one.

Some live a dull way of living very quickly and they are not then certain that they are living a dull way of living. Some live in a sad way of living and are quicker and quicker and they are certain that they are not living in a sad way of living. Some are certain that they would be living in a dreary way of living if they were not so quickly living. Some are trying to be quick in being living and some of them are very quick then and these are living a very tedious way of living.

Some are slow enough and make a sad way of living lose the sadness of that way of living. Some are slow to make a dull way of living fill up to not being such a dull one. Some make themselves a slow one and these then are having a tedious way of living full up with occupation. Some are making themselves slow ones and they are then not such dreary ones in living in a dreary way of living.

Some are coming to know very well that they are living in a very dreary way of living. Some are coming to know very well that they are living in a very sad way of living. Some are coming to know very well that they are living in a very tedious way of living. Some are coming to know very well that they are living in a very dull way of living.

These go shopping. They go shopping and it always was a thing they were rightly doing. Now everything is changing. Certainly everything is changing. They go shopping, they are being in a different way of living. Everything is changing.

Why is everything changing. Everything is changing because the place where they shop is a place where every one is needing to be finding that there are ways of living that are not dreary ones, ways of living that are not sad ones, ways of living that are not dull ones, ways of living that are not tedious ones. Certainly in a way these are existing.

Certainly in a way some are finding a way of living which is not a dull one, which is not a tedious one, which is not a sad one, which is not a dreary one. These are then living in a way of living that is very nearly a completely dreary one, a completely sad one, a completely tedious one, a completely dull one. These are then shopping. Shopping is a thing that is to them, that has been to them a thing that is quite interesting, they are then living in a way of living that is a dreary one, that is a dull one, that is a tedious one, that is in a way a sad one. These are then shopping, certainly shopping is in a way interesting, certainly it is not changing the living they are having, the way of living in which they are living. They are shopping and that is not so interesting and then they are changing in their way of living. They are shopping and slowly they are changing, there is a way of living that is coming then to be in them and it is not completely exciting but it is quite exciting, it is pretty nearly completely exciting. They are living the way they are living, that is a way of living that is a tedious way, that is a sad way, that is a dull way, that is a dreary way and they are living in this way and they are shopping and shopping is not to them very exciting and then it is to them completely exciting and the place where they are shopping is completely existing to those living there in the way they are living, those who are living being ones selling where very many are buying, very many men and very many women, very many women, very many men, very many women.

Some are knowing very well that the living they are living is dull enough, is dreary enough, is tedious enough, is sad enough, yes is sad enough. Some of such of them are changing, very many of such of them are changing, some of such of them are completely changing, very many of such of them are not ever very completely changing. Some of such of them are pretty nearly changing.

Some do not know very well that their way of living is a dull one, is a tedious enough one, is a dreary enough one. Some of such of them are changing, are shopping, some of such of them are shopping and shopping is something, they are shopping and shopping is something but changing is not in being one buying, changing is in being one having some one be one selling something and not selling that thing, changing is then existing, sometimes in some quite some changing, in some quite completely changing, in some some changing, in some not very much changing.

1911

PORTRAIT OF MABEL DODGE AT THE VILLA CURONIA

The days are wonderful and the nights are wonderful and the life is pleasant.

Bargaining is something and there is not that success. The intention is what if application has that accident results are reappearing. They did not darken. That was not an adulteration.

So much breathing has not the same place when there is that much beginning. So much breathing has not the same place when the ending is lessening. So much breathing has the same place and there must not be so much suggestion. There can be there the habit that there is if there is no need of resting. The absence is not alternative.

Any time is the half of all the noise and there is not that disappointment. There is no distraction. An argument is clear.

Packing is not the same when the place which has all that is not emptied. There came there the hall and this was not the establishment. It had not all the meaning.

Blankets are warmer in the summer and the winter is not lonely. This does not assure the forgetting of the intention when there has been and there is every way to send some. There does not happen to be a dislike for water. This is not heartening.

As the expedition is without the participation of the question there will be nicely all that energy. They can arrange that the little color is not bestowed. They can leave it in regaining that intention. It is mostly repaid. There can be an irrigation. They can have the whole paper and they send it in some package. It is not inundated.

A bottle that has all the time to stand open is not so clearly shown when there is green color there. This is not the only way to change it. A little raw potato and then all that softer does happen to show that there has been enough. It changes the expression.

It is not darker and the present time is the best time to agree. This which has been feeling is what has the appetite and the patience and the time to stay. This is not collaborating.

All the attention is when there is not enough to do. This does not determine a question. The only reason that there is not that pressure is that there is a suggestion. There are many going. A delight is not bent. There had been that little wagon. There is that precision when there has not been an imagination. There has not been that kind abandonment. Nobody is alone. If the spread that is not a piece removed from the bed is likely to be whiter then certainly the sprinkling is not drying. There can be the message where the print is pasted and this does not mean that there is that esteem. There can be the likelihood of all the days not coming later and this will not deepen the collected dim version.

It is a gnarled division that which is not any obstruction and the forgotten swelling is certainly attracting, it is attracting the whiter division, it is not sinking to be growing, it is not darkening to be disappearing, it is not aged to be annoying. There can not be sighing. This is this bliss.

Not to be wrapped and then to forget undertaking, the credit and then the resting of that interval, the pressing of the sounding when there is no trinket is not altering, there can be pleasing classing clothing.

A sap that is that adaptation is the drinking that is not increasing. There can be that lack of quivering. That does not originate every invitation. There is not wedding introduction. There is not all that filling. There is the climate that is not existing. There is that plainer. There is the likeliness lying in liking likely likeliness. There is that dispensation. There is the paling that is not reddening, there is the reddening that is not reddening, there is that protection, there is that destruction, there is not the present lessening there is the argument of increasing. There is that that is not that which is that resting. There is not that occupation. There is that particular half of directing that there is that particular whole direction that is not all the measure of any combination. Gliding is not heavily moving. Looking is not vanishing. Laughing is not evaporating. There can be the climax. There can be the same dress. There can be an old dress. There can be the way there is that way there is that which is not that charging what is a regular way of paying. There has been William. All the time is likely. There is the condition. There has been admitting. There is not the print. There is that smiling. There is the season. There is that where there is not that which is where there is what there is which is beguiling. There is a paste.

Abandon a garden and the house is bigger. This is not smiling. This is comfortable. There is the comforting of predilection. An open object is establishing the loss that there was when the vase was not inside the place. It was not wandering.

A plank that was dry was not disturbing the smell of burning and altogether there was the best kind of sitting there could never be all the edging that the largest chair was having. It was not pushed. It moved then. There was not that lifting. There was that which was not any contradiction and there was not the bland fight that did not have that regulation. The contents were not darkening. There was not that hesitation. It was occupied. That was not occupying any exception. Any one had come. There was that distribution.

There was not that velvet spread when there was a pleasant head. The color was paler. The moving regulating is not a distinction. The place is there.

Likely there is not that departure when the whole place that has that texture is so much in the way. It is not there to stay. It does not change that way. A pressure is not later. There is the same. There is not the shame. There is that pleasure.

In burying that game there is not a change of name. There is not perplexing and co-ordination. The toy that is not round has to be found and looking is not straining such relation. There can be that company. It is not wider when the length is not longer and that does make that way of staying away. Every one is exchanging returning. There is not a prediction. The whole day is that way. Any one is resting to say that the time which is not reverberating is acting in partaking.

A walk that is not stepped where the floor is covered is not in the place where the room is entered. The whole one is the same. There is not any stone. There is the wide door that is narrow on the floor. There is all that place.

There is that desire and there is no pleasure and the place is filling the only space that is placed where all the piling is not adjoining. There is not that distraction.

Praying has intention and relieving that situation is not solemn. There comes that way.

The time that is the smell of the plain season is not showing the water is running. There is not all that breath. There is the use of the stone and there is the place of the stuff and there is the practice of expending questioning. There is not that differentiation. There is that which is in time. There is the room that is the largest place when there is all that is where there is space. There is not that perturbation. The legs that show are not the certain ones that have been used. All legs are used. There is no action meant.

The particular space is not beguiling. There is that participation. It is not passing any way. It has that to show. It is why there is no exhalation.

There is all there is when there has all there has where there is what there is. That is what is done when there is done what is done and the union is won and the division is the explicit visit. There is not all of any visit.

1912

SUSIE ASADO

Sweet sweet sweet sweet sweet tea.

    Susie Asado.

Sweet sweet sweet sweet sweet tea.

    Susie Asado.

Susie Asado which is a told tray sure.

A lean on the shoe this means slips slips hers.

When the ancient light grey is clean it is yellow, it is a silver seller.

This is a please this is a please there are the saids to jelly. These are the wets these say the sets to leave a crown to Incy.

Incy is short for incubus.

A pot. A pot is a beginning of a rare bit of trees. Trees tremble, the old vats are in bobbles, bobbles which shade and shove and render clean, render clean must.

    Drink pups.

Drink pups drink pups lease a sash hold, see it shine and a bobolink has pins. It shows a nail.

What is a nail. A nail is unison.

Sweet sweet sweet sweet sweet tea.

1913

PRECIOSILLA

Cousin to Clare washing.

In the win all the band beagles which have cousin lime sign and arrange a weeding match to presume a certain point to exstate to exstate a certain pass lint to exstate a lean sap prime lo and shut shut is life.

Bait, bait tore, tore her clothes, toward it, toward a bit, to ward a sit, sit down in, in vacant surely lots, a single mingle, bait and wet, wet a single establishment that has a lily lily grow. Come to the pen come in the stem, come in the grass grown water.

Lily wet lily wet while. This is so pink so pink in stammer, a long bean which shows bows is collected by a single curly shady, shady get, get set wet bet.

It is a snuff a snuff to be told and have can wither, can is it and sleep sleeps knot, it is a lily scarf the pink and blue yellow, not blue not odor sun, nobles are bleeding

bleeding two seats two seats on end. Why is grief. Grief is strange black. Sugar is melting. We will not swim.

Preciosilla.

Please be please be get, please get wet, wet naturally, naturally in weather. Could it be fire more firier. Could it be so in ate struck. Could it be gold up, gold up stringing, in it while while which is hanging, hanging in dingling, dingling in pinning, not so. Not so dots large dressed dots, big sizes, less laced, less laced diamonds, diamonds white, diamonds bright, diamonds in the in the light, diamonds light diamonds door diamonds hanging to be four, two four, all before, this bean, lessly, all most, a best, willow, vest, a green guest, guest, go go go go go go, go. Go go. Not guessed. Go go.

Toasted susie is my ice-cream.

1913

WHAT HAPPENED

A Five Act Play

ACT ONE

One.

Loud and no cataract. Not any nuisance is depressing.

Five.

A single sum four and five together and one, not any sun a clear signal and an exchange.

Silence is in blessing and chasing and coincidences being ripe. A simple melancholy clearly precious and on the surface and surrounded and mixed strangely. A vegetable window and clearly most clearly an exchange in parts and complete.

A tiger a rapt and surrounded overcoat securely arranged with spots old enough to be thought useful and witty quite witty in a secret and in a blinding flurry.

Length what is length when silence is so windowful. What is the use of a sore if there is no joint and no toady and no tag and not even an eraser. What is the commonest exchange between more laughing and most. Carelessness is carelessness and a cake well a cake is a powder, it is very likely to be powder, it is very likely to be much worse.

A shutter and only shutter and Christmas, quite Christmas, an only shutter and a target a whole color in every center and shooting real shooting and what can hear, that can hear that which makes such an establishment provided with what is provisionary.

Two.

Urgent action is not in graciousness it is not in clocks it is not in water wheels. It is the same so essentially, it is a worry a real worry.

A silence a whole waste of a desert spoon, a whole waste of any little shaving, a whole waste altogether open.

Two.

Paralysis why is paralysis a syllable why is it not more lively.

A special sense a very special sense is ludicrous.

Three.

Suggesting a sage brush with a turkey and also something abominable is not the only pain there is in so much provoking. There is even more. To begin a lecture is a strange way of taking dirty apple blossoms and is there more use in water, certainly there is if there is going to be fishing, enough water would make desert and even prunes, it would make nothing throw any shade because after all is there not more practical humor in a series of photographs and also in a treacherous sculpture.

Any hurry any little hurry has so much subsistence, it has and choosing, it has.

ACT TWO

Three.

Four and nobody wounded, five and nobody flourishing, six and nobody talkative, eight and nobody sensible.

One and a left hand lift that is so heavy that there is no way of pronouncing perfectly.

A point of accuracy, a point of a strange stove, a point that is so sober that the reason left is all the chance of swelling.

The same three.

A wide oak a wide enough oak, a very wide cake, a lightning cooky, a single wide open and exchanged box filled with the same little sac that shines.

The best the only better and more left footed stranger.

The very kindness there is in all lemons oranges apples pears and potatoes.

The same three.

A same frame a sadder portal, a singular gate and a bracketed mischance.

A rich market where there is no memory of more moon than there is everywhere and yet where strangely there is apparel and a whole set.

A connection, a clam cup connection, a survey, a ticket and a return to laying over.

ACT THREE

Two.

A cut, a cut is not a slice, what is the occasion for representing a cut and a slice. What is the occasion for all that.

A cut is a slice, a cut is the same slice. The reason

that a cut is a slice is that if there is no hurry any time is just as useful.

Four.

A cut and a slice is there any question when a cut and a slice are just the same.

A cut and a slice has no particular exchange it has such a strange exception to all that which is different.

A cut and only slice, only a cut and only a slice, the remains of a taste may remain and tasting is accurate.

A cut and an occasion, a slice and a substitute a single hurry and a circumstance that shows that, all this is so reasonable when everything is clear.

One.

All alone with the best reception, all alone with more than the best reception, all alone with a paragraph and something that is worth something, worth almost anything, worth the best example there is of a little occasional archbishop. This which is so clean is precious little when there is no bath water. A long time a very long time there is no use in an obstacle that is original and has a source.

ACT FOUR

Four and four more.

A birthday, what is a birthday, a birthday is a speech, it is a second time when there is tobacco, it is only one time when there is poison. It is more than one time when the occasion which shows an occasional sharp separation is unanimous.

A blanket, what is a blanket, a blanket is so speedy that heat much heat is hotter and cooler, very much cooler almost more nearly cooler than at any other time often.

A blame what is a blame, a blame is what arises and cautions each one to be calm and an ocean and a masterpiece.

A clever saucer, what is a clever saucer, a clever saucer is very likely practiced and even has toes, it has tiny things to shake and really if it were not for a delicate blue color would there be any reason for everyone to differ.

The objection and the perfect central table, the sorrow in borrowing and the hurry in a nervous feeling, the question is it really a plague, is it really an oleander, is it really saffron in color, the surmountable appetite which shows inclination to be warmer, the safety in a match and the safety in a little piece of splinter, the real reason why cocoa is cheaper, the same use for bread as for any breathing that is softer, the lecture and the surrounding large white soft unequal and spread out sale of more and still less is no better, all this makes one regard in a season, one hat in a curtain that in rising higher, one landing and many many more, and many more many more many many more.

ACT FIVE

Two.

A regret a single regret makes a doorway. What is a doorway, a doorway is a photograph.

What is a photograph a photograph is a sight and a sight is always a sight of something. Very likely there is a photograph that gives color if there is then there is that color that does not change any more than it did when there was much more use for photography.

1913

SACRED EMILY

Compose compose beds.

Wives of great men rest tranquil.

Come go stay philip philip.

Egg be takers.

Parts of place nuts.

Suppose twenty for cent.

It is rose in hen.

Come one day.

A firm terrible a firm terrible hindering, a firm hindering have a ray nor pin nor.

Egg in places.

Egg in few insists.

In set a place.

I am not missing.

Who is a permit.

I love honor and obey I do love honor and obey I do.

Melancholy do lip sing.

How old is he.

Murmur pet murmur pet murmur.

Push sea push sea push sea push sea push sea push sea push sea push sea.

Sweet and good and kind to all.

Wearing head.

Cousin tip nicely.

Cousin tip.

Nicely.

Wearing head.

Leave us sit.

I do believe it will finish, I do believe it will finish.

Pat ten patent, Pat ten patent.

Eleven and eighteen.

Foolish is foolish is.

Birds measure birds measure stores birds measure stores measure birds measure.

Exceptional firm bites.

How do you do I forgive you everything and there is nothing to forgive.

Never the less.

Leave it to me.

Weeds without papers.

Weeds without papers are necessary.

Left again left again.

Exceptional considerations.

Never the less tenderness.

Resting cow curtain.

Resting bull pin.

Resting cow curtain.

Resting bull pin.

Next to a frame.

The only hat hair.

Leave us mass leave us. Leave us pass. Leave us. Leave us pass leave us.

Humming is.

No climate.

What is a size.

Ease all I can do.

Colored frame.

Couple of canning.

Ease all I can do.

Humming does as

Humming does as humming is.

What is a size.

No climate.

Ease all I can do.

Shall give it, please to give it.

Like to give it, please to give it.

What a surprise.

Not sooner whether.

Cordially yours.

Pause.

Cordially yours.

Not sooner together.

Cordially yours.

In strewing, in strewing.

That is the way we are one and indivisible.

Pay nuts renounce.

Now without turning around.

I will give them to you to-night.

Cunning is and does cunning is and does the most beautiful notes.

I would like a thousand most most.

Center pricking petunia.

Electrics are tight electrics are white electrics are a button.

Singular pressing.

Recent thimble.

Noisy pearls noisy pearl coat.

Arrange.

Arrange wide opposite.

Opposite it.

Lily ice-cream.

Nevertheless.

A hand is Willie.

Henry Henry Henry.

A hand is Henry.

Henry Henry Henry.

A hand is Willie.

Henry Henry Henry.

All the time.

A wading chest.

Do you mind.

Lizzie do you mind.

Ethel.

Ethel.

Ethel.

Next to barber.

Next to barber bury.

Next to barber bury china.

Next to barber bury china glass.

Next to barber china and glass.

Next to barber and china.

Next to barber and hurry.

Next to hurry.

Next to hurry and glass and china.

Next to hurry and glass and hurry.

Next to hurry and hurry.

Next to hurry and hurry.

Plain cases for see.

Tickle tickle tickle you for education.

A very reasonable berry.

Suppose a selection were reverse.

Cousin to sadden.

A coral neck and a little song so very extra so very Susie.

Cow come out cow come out and out and smell a little.

Draw prettily.

Next to a bloom.

Neat stretch.

Place plenty.

Cauliflower.

Cauliflower.

Curtain cousin.

Apron.

Neither best set.

Do I make faces like that at you.

Pinkie.

Not writing not writing another.

Another one.

Think.

Jack Rose Jack Rose.

Yard.

Practically all of them.

Does believe it.

Measure a measure a measure or.

Which is pretty which is pretty which is pretty.

To be top.

Neglect Waldberg.

Sudden say separate.

So great so great Emily.

Sew grate sew grate Emily.

Not a spell nicely.

Ring.

Weigh pieces of pound.

Aged steps.

Stops.

Not a plan bow.

Why is lacings.

Little slam up.

Cold seam peaches.

Begging to state begging to state begging to state alright.

Begging to state begging to state begging to state alright.

Wheels stows wheels stows.

Wickedness.

Cotton could mere less.

Nevertheless.

Anne.

Analysis.

From the standpoint of all white a week is none too much.

Pink coral white coral, coral coral.

Happy happy happy.

All the, chose.

Is a necessity.

Necessity.

Happy happy happy all the.

Happy happy happy all the.

Necessity.

Remain seated.

Come on come on come on on.

All the close.

Remain seated.

Happy.

All the.

Necessity.

Remain seated.

All the, close.

Websters and mines, websters and mines.

Websters and mines.

Trimming.

Gold space gold space of toes.

Twos, twos.

Pinned to the letter.

In accompany.

In a company in.

Received.

Must.

Natural lace.

Spend up.

Spend up length.

Spend up length.

Length thoroughly.

Neatness.

Neatness Neatness.

Excellent cording.

Excellent cording short close.

Close to.

When.

Pin black.

Cough or up.

Shouting.

Shouting.

Neater pin.

Pinned to the letter.

Was it a space was it a space was it a space to see.

Neither things.

Persons.

Transition.

Say say say.

North of the calender.

Window.

Peoples rest.

Preserve pulls.

Cunning piler.

Next to a chance.

Apples.

Apples.

Apples went.

It was a chance to preach Saturday.

Please come to Susan.

Purpose purpose black.

Extra plain silver.

Furious slippers.

Have a reason.

Have a reason candy.

Points of places.

Neat Nezars.

Which is a cream, can cream.

Ink of paper slightly mine breathes a shoulder able shine.

Necessity.

Near glass.

Put a stove put a stove hoarser.

If I was surely if I was surely.

See girl says.

All the same bright.

Brightness.

When a churn say suddenly when a churn say suddenly.

Poor pour percent.

Little branches.

Pale.

Pale.

Pale.

Pale.

Pale.

Pale.

Pale.

Near sights.

Please sorts.

Example.

Example.

Put something down.

Put something down some day.

Put something down some day in.

Put something down some day in my.

In my hand.

In my hand right.

In my hand writing.

Put something down some day in my hand writing.

Needles less.

Never the less.

Never the less.

Pepperness.

Never the less extra stress.

Never the less.

Tenderness.

Old sight.

Pearls.

Real line.

Shoulders.

Upper states.

Mere colors.

Recent resign.

Search needles.

All a plain all a plain show.

White papers.

Slippers.

Slippers underneath.

Little tell.

I chance.

I chance to.

I chance to to.

I chance to.

What is a winter wedding a winter wedding.

Furnish seats.

Furnish seats nicely.

Please repeat.

Please repeat for.

Please repeat.

This is a name to Anna.

Cushions and pears.

Reason purses.

Reason purses to relay to relay carpets.

Marble is thorough fare.

Nuts are spittoons.

That is a word.

That is a word careless.

Paper peaches.

Paper peaches are tears.

Rest in grapes.

Thoroughly needed.

Thoroughly needed signs.

All but.

Relieving relieving.

Argonauts.

That is plenty.

Cunning saxon symbol.

Symbol of beauty.

Thimble of everything.

Cunning clover thimble.

Cunning of everything.

Cunning of thimble.

Cunning cunning.

Place in pets.

Night town.

Night town a glass.

Color mahogany.

Color mahogany center.

Rose is a rose is a rose is a rose.

Loveliness extreme.

Extra gaiters.

Loveliness extreme.

Sweetest ice-cream.

Page ages page ages page ages.

Wiped Wiped wire wire.

Sweeter than peaches and pears and cream.

Wiped wire wiped wire.

Extra extreme.

Put measure treasure.

Measure treasure.

Tables track.

Nursed.

Dough.

That will do.

Cup or cup or.

Excessively illegitimate.

Pussy pussy pussy what what.

Current secret sneezers.

Ever.

Mercy for a dog.

Medal make medal.

Able able able.

A go to green and a letter spoke a go to green or praise or

Worships worships worships.

Door.

Do or.

Table linen.

Wet spoil.

Wet spoil gaiters and knees and little spools little spools of ready silk lining.

Suppose misses misses.

Curls to butter.

Curls.

Curls.

Settle stretches.

See at till.

Louise.

Sunny.

Sail or.

Sail or rustle.

Mourn in morning.

The way to say.

Patter.

Deal own a.

Robber.

A high b and a perfect sight.

Little things singer.

Jane.

Aiming.

Not in description.

Day way.

A blow is delighted.

1913

ONE

Carl Van Vechten

One.

In the ample checked fur in the back and in the house, in the by next cloth and inner, in the chest, in mean wind.

One.

In the best most silk and water much, in the best most silk.

One.

In the best might last and wind that. In the best might last and wind in the best might last.

Ages, ages, all what sat.

One.

In the gold presently, in the gold presently unsuddenly and decapsized and dewalking.

In the gold coming in.

ONE.

One.

None in stable, none at ghosts, none in the latter spot.

ONE.

One.

An oil in a can, an oil and a vial with a thousand stems. An oil in a cup and a steel sofa.

One.

An oil in a cup and a woolen coin, a woolen card and a best satin.

A water house and a hut to speak, a water house and entirely water, water and water.

TWO.

Two.

A touching white shining sash and a touching white green undercoat and a touching white colored orange and a touching piece of elastic. A touching piece of elastic suddenly.

A touching white inlined ruddy hurry, a touching research in all may day. A touching research is an over show.

A touching expartition is in an example of work, a touching beat is in the best way.

A touching box is in a coach seat so that a touching box is on a coach seat so a touching box is on a coach seat, a touching box is on a coat seat, a touching box is on a coat seat.

A touching box is on the touching so helping held.

Two.

Any left in the touch is a scene, a scene. Any left in is left somehow.

FOUR.

Four.

Four between, four between and hacking. Four between and hacking.

Five.

Four between and a saddle, a kind of dim judge and a great big so colored dog.

1913

ADVERTISEMENTS

I was winsome. Dishonored. And a kingdom. I was not a republic. I was an island and land. I was early to bed. I was a character sodden agreeable perfectly constrained and not artificial. I was relieved by contact. I said good morning, good evening, hour by hour. I said one had power. I said I was frequently troubled. I can be fanciful. They have liberal ideas. They have dislikes. I dread smoke. Where are there many children. Where are there many children. We have an account. We count Daisy. Daisy is a daughter. Her name is Antonia. She is pleased to say what will you have. Horns and horns. Nicholas is not a stranger. Neither is Monica. No one is a stranger. We refuse to greet anyone. We like Genevieve to satisfy us. I do not like what I am saying.

How can you describe a trip. It is so boastful.

He said definitely that they would. They have. It's a little late. I hope the other things will be as he states them. I have confidence. I have not eaten peaches. Yes I have. I apologize. I did not want to say the other word that was red. You know what I mean.

Why can I read it if I know page to page what is coming if I have not read it before. Why can I read it. I do.

I didn't.

Let me see. I wish to tell about the door. The door opens before the kitchen. The kitchen is closed. The other door is open and that makes a draft. This is very pleasant in summer. We did not expect the weather to change so suddenly. There seem to be more mosquitoes than ever. I don't understand why I like narrative so much to read. I do like it. I see no necessity for disclosing particularity I am mightily disturbed by a name such as an English home. An English home is beautiful. So are the times.

A dog does not bark when he hears other dogs bark. He sleeps carefully he does not know about it. I am not pained.

This is the narrative. In watching a balloon, a kite, a boat, steps and watches, any kind of a call is remarkable remarkably attuned. A resemblance to Lloyd George, bequeathing prayers, saying there is no hope, having a french meeting. Jenny said that she said that she did not believe in her country. Anyone who does not believe in her country speaks the truth. How dare you hurt the other with canes. I hope he killed him. Read it. I believe Bulgaria. I have pledges. I have relief.

I AM NOT PATIENT

I am interested. In that table. I like washing gates with a mixture. We get it by bringing up melons. White melons have a delicious flavor.

I am not patient. I get angry at a dog. I do not wish to hear a noise. I did not mind the noise which the client made. I wished to see the pearls. How easily we ask for what we are going to have. By this we are pleased and excited.

The hope there is is that we will hear the news. We are all elated. Did you see her reading the paper. I cannot help wanting to write a story.

A woman who had children and called to them making them hear singing is a match for the man who has one child and does not tell him to play there with children. Heaps of them are gambling. They tell about stitches. Stitches are easily made in hot weather and vegetation. Tube roses are famous.

I could be so pleased. It would please me if Van would mention it. Why is an index dear to him. He has thousands of gesticulations. He can breathe.

White and be a Briton. This means a woman from the north of France. They are very religious. They say blue is not a water color. It should be a bay. We are pleased with her. She washes her hair very often.

Do not tremble. If she had an institution it is the one excluding her mother. Her native land is not beautiful. She likes the poet to mutter. He does. The olive.

We had that impression. Do speak. Have they been able to arrange matters with the proprietor.

I will not please play. I will adorn the station. It has extraordinarily comfortable seats.

TO OPEN

Not too long for leading, not opening his mouth and sitting. Not bequeathing butter. Butter comes from Brittany. In the summer it smells rancid. We do not like it. We have ceased use of it. We find that oil does as well. We can mix oil with butter but we have lard. We use lard altogether. We prefer it to butter. We use the butter in winter. We have not been using it before the winter. We mix lard and oil. We will use butter.

DO LET US BE FAITHFUL AND TRUE

I do not wish to see I do not wish to see Harry I do not wish to see Harry Brackett I do not wish to see Harry Brackett.

A GRAPE CURE

What did we have for dinner we had a melon lobster chicken then beet salad and fruit. How can you tell a melon. You tell it by weight and pressing it. You do not make mistakes. We are pleased with it. Do we like a large dog. Not at all.

BATTLE

Battle creek. I was wet. All the doors showed light. It is strange how Brittany is not attractive as Mallorca and yet butter does make a difference. We are perfect creatures. What is a festival. Saturday to some. Not to be dishonored. Not to be tall and dishonored they usually aren't but some are, some are tall and dishonored. By this I mean that coming down the mountain faces which are shining are reflecting the waving of the boat which is there now. I distrust everybody. Do sleep well. Everywhere there is a cat. We will leave by boat. I am not pleased with this. I will get so that I can write a story.

FASTENING TUBE ROSES

I understand perfectly well how to fix an electric fan. Of course it makes sparks but when the two black pieces that do not come together are used up you get this. I do it without any bother. I am not certain I could learn it. It is not difficult. We do not find that it does away with mosquitoes. We use it in the night. Sundays there is no electricity.

THEY DO IT BETTER THAN I DO

I can. I can be irritated. I hate lizards when you call them crocodile. She screamed. She screamed. I do not know why I am irritated.

IT IS A NATURAL THING

Do not do that again. I do not like it. Please give it away. We will not take it to Paris. I do not want the gas stove. It has a round oven. It does not bake. We use coal by preference. It is very difficult not to bathe in rain water. Rain water is so delicious. It is boiled. We boil it.

LOUD LETTERS

Look up and not down.

Look right and not left.

And lend a hand.

We were so pleased with the Mallorcans and the wind and the party. They were so good to offer us ice-cream. They do not know the french names.

Isn't it peculiar that those that fear a thunder storm are willing to drink water again and again, boiled water because it is healthy. All the water is in cisterns rain water. There are no vegetables that is to say no peas. There are plenty of beets. I like them so much. So do I melons. I was so glad that this evening William came and ate some. It would not go back as if it hadn't been good.

PLEASURES IN SINCERE WISHES

I wish you to enjoy these cigarettes. They are a change from those others. I understand that you had some very good ones. You are not able to get these any more. I have tried to get them. They tell me that they cannot say when they will come. They do not know that about them. We sleep easily. We are awakened by the same noise. It is so disagreeable.

AN EXHIBITION

I do not quite succeed in making an exhibition. Please place me where there is air. I like to be free. I like to be sure that the dogs will not be worried. I don't see how they can avoid crickets. They come in. They are so bothersome. We must ask Polybe to wish.

THE BOAT

I was so disappointed in the boat. It was larger than the other. It did not have more accommodation. It made the noise which was disagreeable. I feel that I would have been willing to say that I liked it very well if I had not seen it when it was painted. It is well never to deceive me.

THREADNEEDLE STREET

I am going to conquer. I am going to be flourishing. I am going to be industrious. Please forgive me everything.

PRESENT

This is a ceremonial. When you are bashful you do not think. When a present is offered you accept it you accept the bracelet worn by the nun so that it rusted. You do not know what to do with it. You describe its qualities. It is a pleasure to have it. You will give it. You are steadily tender. You say the beginning is best. Why do you say Englishman. You say Englishman because he wished it. Do not hurry.

EVIAN WATER

Evian water is very good. Sometimes I am not sure it is put up by them at least now when there is a war. I say it is fresh. When I do not like a bottle I throw it away. I throw the water away.

1916

LADIES' VOICES

Curtain Raiser

Ladies' voices give pleasure.

The acting two is easily led. Leading is not in winter. Here the winter is sunny.

Does that surprise you.

Ladies voices together and then she came in.

Very well good night.

Very well good night Mrs. Cardillac.

That's silver.

You mean the sound.

Yes the sound.

ACT II.

Honest to God Miss Williams I don't mean to say that I was older.

But you were.

Yes I was. I do not excuse myself. I feel that there is no reason for passing an archduke.

You like the word.

You know very well that they all call it their house.

As Christ was to Lazarus so was the founder of the hill to Mahon.

You really mean it.

I do.

ACT III.

Yes Genevieve does not know it. What. That we are seeing Caesar.

Caesar kisses.

Kisses to-day.

Caesar kisses every day.

Genevieve does not know that it is only in this country that she could speak as she does.

She does speak very well doesn't she. She told them that there was not the slightest intention on the part of her countrymen to eat the fish that was not caught in their country.

In this she was mistaken.

ACT IV.

What are ladies voices.

Do you mean to believe me.

Have you caught the sun.

Dear me have you caught the sun.

SCENE II.

Did you say they were different I said it made no difference.

Where does it. Yes.

Mr. Richard Sutherland. This is a name I know.

Yes.

The Hotel Victoria.

Many words spoken to me have seemed English.

Yes we do hear one another and yet what are called voices the best decision in telling of balls.

Masked balls.

Yes masked balls.

Poor Augustine.

1916

ACCENTS IN ALSACE

A Reasonable Tragedy

Scene Mulhouse

ACT I. THE SCHEMILS.

Brother brother go away and stay.

Sister mother believe me I say.

They will never get me as I run away.

He runs away and stays away and strange to say he passes the lines and goes all the way and they do not find him but hear that he is there in the foreign legion in distant Algier.

And what happens to the family.

The family manages to get along and then some one of his comrades in writing a letter which is gotten hold of by the Boche find he is a soldier whom they cannot touch, so what do they do they decide to embrew his mother and sister and father too. And how did they escape by paying somebody money.

That is what you did with the Boche. You always paid some money to some one it might be a colonel or it might be a sergeant but anyway you did it and it was necessary so then what happened.

THE SCHEMMELS.

Sing so la douse so la dim.
Un deux trois
Can you tell me wha
Is it indeed.
What you call a Petide.
And then what do I say to thee
Let me kiss thee willingly.
Not a mountain not a goat not a door.
Not a whisper not a curl not a gore
In me meeney miney mo.
You are my love and I tell you so.
   In the daylight
   And the night
Baby winks and holds me tight.
In the morning and the day and the evening and alway.
I hold my baby as I say.

Completely.
And what is an accent of my wife.
And accent and the present life.
Oh sweet oh my oh sweet oh my
I love you love you and I try
I try not to be nasty and hasty and good
I am my little baby's daily food.

ALSATIA.

In the exercise of greatness there is charm.
Believe me I mean to do you harm.
And except you have a stomach to alarm.
I mean to scatter so you are to arm.
Let me go.
And the Alsatians say.
What has another prince a birthday.

Now we come back to the Schimmels.
Schimmel Schimmel Gott in Himmel
Gott in Himmel There comes Shimmel.
Schimmel is an Alsatian name.

ACT II.

It is a little thing to expect nobody to sell what you give them.

It is a little thing to be a minister.

It is a little thing to manufacture articles.

All this is modest.

THE BROTHER.

Brother brother here is mother.

We are all very well.

SCENE.

Listen to thee sweet cheerie
Is the pleasure of me.
In the way of being hungry and tired
That is what a depot makes you
A depot is not for trains
Its for us.
What are baby carriages
Household goods

And not the dears.
But dears.

ANOTHER ACT.

Clouds do not fatten with teaching.
They do not fatten at all.
We wonder if it is influence
By this way I guess.
She said. I like it better than Eggland.
What do you mean.
We never asked how many children over eleven.
You cannot imagine what I think about the country.
Any civilians killed.

ACT II.

See the swimmer. He don't swim.
See the swimmer.
My wife is angry when she sees a swimmer.

OPENING II.

We like Hirsing.

III.

We like the mayor of Guebwiller.

IV.

We like the road between Cernay and the railroad.
We go everywhere by automobile.

ACT II.

This is a particular old winter.
Everybody goes back.
Back.
I can clean.
I can clean.
I cannot clean without a change in birds.
I am so pleased that they cheat.

ACT 54.

In silver stars and red crosses.

In paper money and water.

We know a french wine.

Alsatian wine is dearer.

They are not particularly old.

Old men are old.

There are plenty to hear of Schemmel having appendicitis.

SCENE II.

Can you mix with another

Can you be a Christian and a Swiss.

Mr. Zumsteg. Do I hear a saint.

Louisa. They call me Lisela.

Mrs. Zumsteg. Are you going to hear me.

Young Mr. Zumsteg. I was looking at the snow.

All of them. Like flowers. They like flowers.

SCENE III.

It is an occasion.

When you see a Hussar.

A Zouave.

A soldier

An antiquary.

Perhaps it is another.

We were surprised with the history of Marguerite's father and step-father and the American Civil War.

Joseph. Three three six, six, fifty, six fifty, fifty, seven.

Reading french.

Reading french.

Reading french singing.

Any one can look at pictures.

They explain pictures.

The little children have old birds.

They wish they were women.

Any one can hate a Prussian.

Alphonse what is your name.

Henri what is your name.

Madeleine what is your name.

Louise what is your name.

René what is your name.

Berthe what is your name.

Charles what is your name.

Marguerite what is your name.

Jeanne what is your name.

ACT 425.

We see a river and we are glad to say that that is in a way in the way to-day.

We see all the windows and we see a souvenir and we see the best flower. The flower of the truth.

AN INTERLUDE.

Thirty days in April gave a chance to sing at a wedding.

Three days in February gave reality to life.

Fifty days every year do not make subtraction.

The Alsatians sing anyway.

Forty days in September.

Forty days in September we know what it is to spring.

ACT IN AMERICA.

Alsatians living in America.

FEBRUARY XIV.

On this day the troops who had been at Mulhouse came again.

They came in the spring.

The spring is late in Alsace.

Water was good and hot anyway.

What are you doing.

Making music and burning the surface of marble.

When the surface of marble is burned it is not much discolored.

No but there is a discussion.

And then the Swiss.

What is amiss.

The Swiss are the origin of Mulhouse.

ALSACE OR ALSATIANS.

We have been deeply interested in the words of the song.

The Alsatians do not sing as well as their storks.

Their storks are their statuettes.

The rule is that angels and food and eggs are all sold by the dozen.

We were astonished.

And potatoes

Potatoes are eaten dry.

This reminds me of another thing I said. A woman likes to use money.

And if not.

She feels it really is her birthday.

Is it her birthday.

God bless it is her birthday.

Please carry me to Danemarie.

And what does Herbstadt say.

The names of cities are the names of all.

And pronouncing villages is more of a test than umbrella.

This was the first thing we heard in Alsatia.

Canary, roses, violets and curtains and bags and churches and rubber tires and an examination.

All the leaves are green and babyish.

How many children make a family.

THE WATCH ON THE RHINE.

Sweeter than water or cream or ice. Sweeter than bells of roses. Sweeter than winter or summer or spring. Sweeter than pretty posies. Sweeter than anything is my queen and loving is her nature.

Loving and good and delighted and best is her little King and Sire whose devotion is entire who has but one desire to express the love which is hers to inspire.

In the photograph the Rhine hardly showed

In what way do chimes remind you of singing. In what way do birds sing. In what way are forests black or white.

We saw them blue.

With for get me nots.

In the midst of our happiness we were very pleased.

1919

A MOVIE

Eyes are a surprise
Printzess a dream
Buzz is spelled with z
Fuss is spelled with s
So is business.
The UNITED STATES is comical.
Now I want to tell you about the Monroe doctrine.
We think very nicely we think very well of the Monroe
doctrine.

American painter painting in French country near
railroad track. Mobilisation locomotive passes with
notification for villages.

Where are American tourists to buy my pictures sacre
nom d'un pipe says the american painter.

American painter sits in café and contemplates empty
pocket book as taxi cabs file through Paris carrying

French soldiers to battle of the Marne. I guess I'll be a taxi driver here in gay Paree says the american painter.

Painter sits in studio trying to learn names of streets with help of Brettonne peasant femme de menage. He becomes taxi driver. Ordinary street scenes in war time Paris.

Being lazy about getting up in the mornings he spends some of his dark nights in teaching Brettonne femme de menage peasant girl how to drive the taxi so she can replace him when he wants to sleep.

America comes into the war american painter wants to be american soldier. Personnel officer interviews him. What have you been doing, taxiing. You know Paris, Secret Service for you go on taxiing.

He goes on taxiing and he teaches Brettonne f. m. english so she can take his place if need be.

One night he reads his paper under the light. Police man tells him to move up, don't want to wants to read.

Man comes up wants to go to the station.

Painter has to take him. Gets back, reading again.

Another man comes wants to go to the station. Painter takes him.

Comes back to read again. Two american officers come up. Want to go to the station.

Painter says Tired of the station take you to Berlin if you like. No station.

Officers say Give you a lot if you take us outside town on way to the south, first big town.

He says alright got to stop at home first to get his coat.

Stops at home calls out to Brettonne f. m. Get busy telegraph to all your relations, you have them all over, ask have you any american officers staying forever. Be back to-morrow.

Back to-morrow. Called up by chief secret service. Goes to see him. Money has been disappearing out of quartermaster's department in chunks. You've got a free hand. Find out something.

Goes home. Finds f. m. brettonne surrounded with telegrams and letters from relatives. Americans everywhere but everywhere. She groans. Funny americans everywhere but everywhere they all said. Many funny americans everywhere. Two americans not so funny here my fifth cousin says, she is helping in the hospital at Avignon. Such a sweet american soldier. So young so tall so tender. Not very badly hurt but will stay a long

long time. He has been visited by american officers who live in a villa. Two such nice ladies live there too and they spend and they spend, they buy all the good sweet food in Avignon. "Is that something William Sir," says the brettonne f. m.

Its snowing but no matter we will get there in the taxi. Take us two days and two nights you inside and me out. Hurry. They start, the funny little taxi goes over the mountains with and without assistance, all tired out he is inside, she driving when they turn down the hill into Avignon. Just then two americans on motor cycles come on and Brettonne f.m. losing her head grand smash. American painter wakes up burned, he sees the two and says by God and makes believe he is dead. The two are very helpful. A team comes along and takes american painter and all to hospital. Two americans ride off on motor cycles direction of Nimes and Pont du Gard.

Arrival at hospital, interview with the wounded american who described two american officers who had been like brothers to him, didn't think any officer could be so chummy with a soldier. Took me out treated me, cigarettes, everything fine.

Where have they gone on to, to Nimes.

Yes Pont du Gard.

American painter in bed in charge of french nursing nun but manages to escape and leave for Pont du Gard in mended taxi. There under the shadow of that imperishable monument of the might and industry of ancient Rome exciting duel. French gendarme american painter, taxi, f. m. brettonne, two american crooks with motor cycles on which they try to escape over the top of the Pont du Gard, great stunt, they are finally captured. They have been the receivers of the stolen money.

After many other adventures so famous has become the american painter, Brettonne femme de menage and taxi that in the march under the arch at the final triumph of the allies the taxi at the special request of General Pershing brings up the rear of the procession after the tanks, the Brettonne driving and the american painter inside waving the american flag Old Glory and the tricolor.

CURTAIN

1920

A SAINT IN SEVEN

I thought perhaps that we would win by human means, I knew we could win if we did win but I did not think that we could win by human means, and now we have won by human means.

A saint followed and not surrounded.

LIST OF PERSONAGES

1. A saint with a lily.

Second. A girl with a rooster in front of her and a bush of strange flowers at her side and a small tree behind her.

3. A guardian of a museum holding a cane.

4. A woman leaning forward.

5. A woman with a sheep in front of her a small tree behind her.

6. A woman with black hair and two bundles one under each arm.

7. A night watchman of a hotel who does not fail to stand all the time.

8. A very stout girl with a basket and flowers summer flowers and the flowers are in front of a small tree.

SAINTS IN SEASON

See Saints in seven.

And how do royalists accuse themselves.

Saints.

Saint Joseph.

In pleading sadness length of sadness in pleading length of sadness and no sorrow. No sorrow and no sadness length of sadness.

A girl addresses a bountiful supply of seed to feed a chicken. Address a bountiful supply of trees to shade them. Address a bountiful supply to them.

A guardian.

In days and nights beside days are followed by daisies. We find them and they find them and water finds them and they grow best where we meant to suggest.

We suggested that we would go there again. A woman leaning forward.

She was necessarily taken to be no taller.

A girl.

If she may say what she will say she will say that there were a quantity of voices and they were white and then darker.

A woman with two bundles.

If she did it to be useful if she did not even attract the same throne. What did I say Did royalists say that they did not have this to say to-day.

Standing.

Measure an alarm by refusing to alarm them and they shone this not as a disaster but as a pretension. Do you pretend to be unfavorable to their thought.

Eighth.

If you hold heavily heavily instead. Instead of in there. Did you not intend to show this to them.

Saint.

A Saint.

Saint and very well I thank you.

Two in bed.

Two in bed.

Yes two in bed.

They had eaten.

Two in bed.

They had eaten.

Two in bed.

She says weaken

If she said.

She said two in bed.

She said they had eaten.

She said yes two in bed.

She said weaken.

Do not acknowledge to me that seven are said that a Saint and seven that it is said that a saint in seven that there is said to be a saint in seven.

Now as to illuminations.

They are going to illuminate and every one is to put into their windows their most beautiful object and every one will say and the streets will be crowded everyone will say look at it. They do say look at it.

To look at it. They will look at it. They will say look at it.

If it should rain they will all be there. If it should be windy they will all be there. Who will be there. They will all be there.

Names of streets named after the saint. Names of places named after the saint. Names of saints named after the saint. Names of sevens named after the saint. The saints in sevens.

Noon-light for Roman arches.

He left fairly early.

Let them make this seen.

Louise giggled.

Michael was not angry nor was he stuttering nor was he able to silence them. He was angry he was stuttering and he was able to answer them.

They were nervous.

Josephine was able to be stouter. Amelia was really not repaid.

And the taller younger and weaker older and straighter one said come to eat again.

Michael was not able to come angrily to them. He angrily muttered for them.

Louise was separated to Heloise and not by us. So then you see saints for them.

Louise.

Heloise.

Amelia.

Josephine.

Michael and Elinor.

Seven, a saint in seven and in this way it was not Paul. Paul was deprived of nothing. Saint in seven a saint in seven.

Who.

A saint in seven.

Owls and bees.

If you please.

Paul makes honey and orange trees.

Michael makes coal and celery.

Louise makes rugs and reasonably long.

Heloise makes the sea and she settles well away from it.

Amelia does not necessarily please. She does not place herself near linen.

Josephine measures a little toy and she may be no neater.

Eleanor has been more satisfied and feeble. She does not look as able to stay nor does she seem as able to go any way.

Saints in seven makes italics sombre.

I make fun of him of her.

I make fun of them.

They make fun of them of this. They make fun of him of her.

She makes fun of of them of him.

He makes fun of them of her.

They make fun of her.

He makes fun of them.

She makes fun of him.

I make fun of them.

We have made them march. She has made a procession.

A saint in seven and there were six. A saint in seven and there were eight. A saint in seven.

If you know who pleads who precedes who succeeds.

He leads.

He leads and they follow. One two three four and as yet there are no more.

A saint in seven.

And when do they sleep again. A ring around the moon is seen to follow the moon and the moon is in the center of the ring and the ring follows the moon.

Sleeping, to-day sleeping to-day is nearly a necessity and to-day coals reward the five. One two three four five.

Corals reward the five. In this way they are not leaning with the intention of being a hindrance to satisfaction.

A saint in seven is told of bliss.

I will know why they open so.

Carefully seen to be safely arranged.

One two three four five six seven. A saint in seven.

To begin in this way.

Carefully attended carefully attended to this.

If we had seen if they had seen if we had seen what was in between, they went very slowly so that we might know but to be slow and we were not slow and to show and they showed it and we did not decide because we had already come to a decision.

Saints in seven are a very large number. Seven and seven is not as pretty as five and five. And five and five need not mean more. Now to remember how to mean to be gay. Gayly the boxer the boxer very gayly depresses no one. He seems he does seem he dreams he does dream he seems to dream.

Extra readiness to recall himself to these places. Thanks so much for startling. Do not by any means start to worship in order to be excellent. He is excellent again and again.

A saint can share expenses he can share and he can be interested in their place. Their place is plentifully sprinkled as they bend forward. And no one does mean to contend any more.

A saint in seven plentifully.

None of it is good.

It has been said that the woods are the poor man's overcoat but we have found the mountains which are near by and not high can be an overcoat to us. Can he be an overcoat to us.

A saint in seven wished to be convinced by us that the mountains near by and not high can give protection from the wind. One does not have to consider rain because it cannot rain here. A saint in seven wishes to be convinced by us that the mountains which are near by would act as a protection to those who find it cold and yet when one considers that nothing is suffering neither men women children lambs roses and broom, broom is yellow when one considers that neither broom, roses lambs men children and women none of them suffer neither here nor in the mountains near by the mountains are not high and if it were not true that every one had to be sure that they were there every one would be persuaded that they had persuaded that they had been persuaded that this was true.

He told us that he knew that the name was the same. A saint in seven can declare this to be true.

He comes again. Yes he comes again and what does he say he says do you know this do you refuse no more than you give. That is the way to spell it do you refuse no more than you give.

He searches for more than one word. He manages to eat finally and as he does so and as he does so and as he does so he manages to cut the water in two. If water is flowing down a canal and it is understood that the canal is full if the canal has many outlets for irrigation purposes and the whole country is irrigated if even the mountains are irrigated by the canal and in this way neither oil nor seeds nor wood is needed and it is needed by them why then do the examples remain here examples of industry of cowardice of pleasure of reasonable sight seeing of objections and of lands and oceans. We do not know oceans. We do not know measures. Measure and measure and then decide that a servant beside, what is a servant beside. No one knows how easily he can authorise him to go, how easily she can authorise her to go how easily they can authorise them to come and to go. I authorise you to come and go. I authorise you to go. I authorise you to go and come.

1922

IDEM THE SAME

A Valentine to Sherwood Anderson

I knew too that through them I knew too that he was through, I knew too that he threw them. I knew too that they were through, I knew too I knew too, I knew I knew them.

I knew to them.

If they tear a hunter through, if they tear through a hunter, if they tear through a hunt and a hunter, if they tear through the different sizes of the six, the different sizes of the six which are these, a woman with a white package under one arm and a black package under the other arm and dressed in brown with a white blouse, the second Saint Joseph the third a hunter in a blue coat and black garters and a plaid cap, a fourth a knife grinder who is full faced and a very little woman with black hair and a yellow hat and an excellently smiling appropriate soldier. All these as you please.

In the meantime examples of the same lily. In this way please have you rung.

WHAT DO I SEE.

A very little snail.
A medium sized turkey.
A small band of sheep.
A fair orange tree.
All nice wives are like that.
Listen to them from here.
Oh.
You did not have an answer.
Here.
Yes.

A VERY VALENTINE.

Very fine is my valentine.
Very fine and very mine.
Very mine is my valentine very mine and very fine.
Very fine is my valentine and mine, very fine very mine and mine is my valentine.

WHY DO YOU FEEL DIFFERENTLY.

Why do you feel differently about a very little snail and a big one.

Why do you feel differently about a medium sized turkey and a very large one.

Why do you feel differently about a small band of sheep and several sheep that are riding.

Why do you feel differently about a fair orange tree and one that has blossoms as well.

Oh very well.

All nice wives are like that.

To Be
No Please.
To Be
They can please
Not to be
Do they please.
Not to be
Do they not please
Yes please.

Do they please
No please.
Do they not please
No please.
Do they please.
Please.
If you please.
And if you please.
And if they please
And they please.
To be pleased
Not to be pleased.
Not to be displeased.
To be pleased and to please.

KNEELING

One two three four five six seven eight nine and ten.

The tenth is a little one kneeling and giving away a rooster with this feeling.

I have mentioned one, four five seven eight and nine.

Two is also giving away an animal.

Three is changed as to disposition.

Six is in question if we mean mother and daughter, black and black caught her, and she offers to be three she offers it to me.

That is very right and should come out below and just so.

BUNDLES FOR THEM.
A HISTORY OF GIVING BUNDLES.

We were able to notice that each one in a way carried a bundle, they were not a trouble to them nor were they all bundles as some of them were chickens some of them pheasants some of them sheep and some of them bundles, they were not a trouble to them and then indeed we learned that it was the principal recreation and they were so arranged that they were not given away, and to-day they were given away.

I will not look at them again.

They will not look for them again.

They have not seen them here again.

They are in there and we hear them again.

In which way are stars brighter than they are. When we have come to this decision. We mention many thousands of buds. And when I close my eyes I see them.

If you hear her snore
It is not before you love her
You love her so that to be her beau is very lovely
She is sweetly there and her curly hair is very lovely
She is sweetly here and I am very near and that is very lovely.

She is my tender sweet and her little feet are stretched out well which is a treat and very lovely

Her little tender nose is between her little eyes which close and are very lovely.

She is very lovely and mine which is very lovely.

ON HER WAY.

If you can see why she feels that she kneels if you can see why he knows that he shows what he bestows, if you can see why they share what they share, need we question that there is no doubt that by this time if they had intended to come they would have sent some notice of such intention. She and they and indeed the decision itself is not early dissatisfaction.

IN THIS WAY.

Keys please, it is useless to alarm any one it is useless to alarm some one it is useless to be alarming and to get fertility in gardens in salads in heliotrope and in dishes. Dishes and wishes are mentioned and dishes and wishes are not capable of darkness. We like sheep. And so does he.

LET US DESCRIBE.

Let us describe how they went. It was a very windy night and the road although in excellent condition and extremely well graded has many turnings and although the curves are not sharp the rise is considerable. It was a very windy night and some of the larger vehicles found it more prudent not to venture. In consequence some of those who had planned to go were unable to do so. Many others did go and there was a sacrifice, of what shall we, a sheep, a hen, a cock, a village, a ruin, and all that and then that having been blessed let us bless it.

1922

CEZANNE

The Irish lady can say, that to-day is every day. Caesar can say that every day is to-day and they say that every day is as they say.

In this way we have a place to stay and he was not met because he was settled to stay. When I said settled I meant settled to stay. When I said settled to stay I meant settled to stay Saturday. In this way a mouth is a mouth. In this way if in as a mouth if in as a mouth where, if in as a mouth where and there. Believe they have water too. Believe they have that water too and blue when you see blue, is all blue precious too, is all that that is precious too is all that and they meant to absolve you. In this way Cezanne nearly did nearly in this way Cezanne nearly did nearly did and nearly did. And was I surprised. Was I very surprised. Was I surprised. I was surprised and in that patient, are you patient when you find bees. Bees in a garden make a specialty of honey and so does honey. Honey and prayer. Honey and there. There where the grass can grow nearly four times yearly.

1923

A BOOK CONCLUDING
WITH AS A WIFE HAS A COW

A Love Story

KEY TO CLOSET.

There is a key.

There is a key to a closet that opens the drawer. And she keeps both so that neither money nor candy will go suddenly, Fancy, baby, new year. She keeps both so that neither money nor candy will go suddenly, Fancy baby New Year, fancy baby mine, fancy.

HAPPEN TO HAVE.

She does happen to have an aunt and in visiting and in taking a flower she shows that she is well supplied with sweet food at home otherwise she would have taken candies to her aunt as it would have been her sister. Her sister did.

RIGHT AWAY.

Active at a glance and said, said it again. Active at a glance and then to change gold right away. Active at a glance and not to change gold right away.

FISH.

Can fish be wives and wives and wives and have as many as that. Can fish be wives and have as many as that.

Ten o'clock or earlier.

PINK.

Pink looks as pink, pink looks as pink, as pink as pink supposes, suppose.

QUICKLY.

She will finish first and come, the second time she will finish first and come. The second time.

DECISION.

He decided when he had a house he would not buy them. By and by. By then.

CHOOSE.

He let it be expected and he let it be expected and she let it be expected and he came and brought them and she did not. Usually she sent them and usually he brought them. They were well-chosen.

HAD A HORSE.

If in place of a nose she had a horse and in place of a flower she had wax and in place of a melon she had a stone and in place of perfume buckles how many days would it be.

JULIA.

She asked for white and it was refused, she asked for pink and it was refused she asked for white and pink and it was agreed, it was agreed it would be pink and it was agreed to.

A COUSIN.

If a mistake as to the other if in mistake as to the brother, if by mistake and it was either if and all of it came and come. To come means partly that.

LOOK LIKE.

Look like look like it and he had twenty and more than twenty of them too. The great question is is it easier to have more than were wanted and in that case what do they do with it.

TO-DAY.

Yesterday not at all. To-day one to each one of four, ten to one two to one fifty to one and none to one. And might be satisfied. So also is the one who not being forgotten had five.

LONGER.

She stayed away longer.

BESIDE.

It can be known that he changed from Friday to Sunday. It can also be known that he changed from year to year. It can also be known that he was worried. It can also be known that his fellow-voyager would not only be attentive but would if necessary forget to come. Everybody would be grateful.

IN QUESTION.

How large a mouth has a good singer. He knows. How much better is one color than another. He knows. How far away is a city from a city. He knows. How often is it delayed. He knows.

MUCH LATER.

Elephants and birds of beauty and a gold-fish. Gold fish or a superstition. They always bring bad luck. He had them and he was not told. Gold fish and he was not old. Gold fish and he was not to scold. Gold fish all told. The result was that the other people never had them and he knew nothing of it.

NEGLECTED AND NEGLECTFUL.

She needed it all very well and pressed her, she needed it all very well and as read, to read it better a letter and better, to read it and let her it all very well.

AND SOUP.

It has always been a test of who made it best, and it has always been a test and who made it best. Who made it best it has always been a test. It has always been a test it has always been a test. Who made it best. Who made it best it has always been a test.

PETER.

Peter said Peter said eyes are always and eyes are always. Peter said Peter said, eyes are always and Peter said eyes are always. Peter said eyes are always.

Peter said eyes are always.

EMILY.

Emily is admitted admittedly, Emily is admittedly Emily is admittedly.

Emily said Emily said, Emily is admittedly Emily. Emily said Emily is admittedly is Emily said Emily is admittedly Emily said Emily is Emily is admittedly.

JULIA AGNES AND EMILY.

Emily is and Julia. Julia is and Agnes. Agnes will entertain Julia. Emily is and Agnes is and will entertain Julia and Agnes will entertain Julia Agnes will entertain Julia.

THERE.

There is an excuse for expecting success there is an excuse. There is an excuse for expecting success and there is an excuse for expecting success. And at once.

IN ENGLISH.

Even in the midst and may be even in the midst and even in the midst and may be. Watched them.

THEY HAD.

They had no children. They had no children but three sister-in-laws a brother which brother and no nephews and no nieces and no other language.

IN ADDITION.

They think that they will they think that they will change their opinion concerning. And it is nearly what they said.

Could and could she be in addition.

THESE.

Three mentioned the three mentioned are too much glass too many hyacinths too many horses. Horses are used at once. Why are horses used at once.

A LITTLE BEGINNING.

She says it is a small beginning, she says that partly this and partly that, she says it is partly this and partly that, she says that it is what she is accustomed to.

INTRODUCTION.

When they introduced not at all when they introduced not at all.

A SLATE.

A long time in which to decide that although it is a slate a slate used to mean a slate pencil.

PLACES.

If he came and was at once inclined inclined to have heard that how many places are there in it. How many places are there in it.

IN ENGLISH.

Longer legs than English. In English longer legs than English.

IN HALF.

Half the size of that. This does not refer to a half or a whole or a piece. Half the size of that refers only to the size.

NOT SURPRISING.

It is not at all surprising. Not at all surprising. If he gets it done at all. It is not at all surprising.

HANDS AND GRATEFUL.

Hands and grateful. This does enjoying this. Hands and grateful very grateful. Go upstairs go upstairs go upstairs go. Hands and grateful.

SUSPICIONS.

He was suspicious of it and he had every reason to be suspicious of it.

AN AID TO MEMORY.

In aid of memory. Mentioned by itself alone. Butter or flattery. Mentioned by itself. In aid of memory mentioned by itself alone.

ALL.

He was the last and best of all not at all. He was the last of all he was the best of all he was the last and best of all not at all.

FANCY.

Fancy looking at it now and if it resembled he made half of it.

A TRAIT.

He met him. It was very difficult to remember who was here alone.

This decided us to consider it a trait.

READY.

When I was as ready to like it as ever I was ready to account for the difference between and the flowers.

Are you ready yet, not yet.

KNIVES.

Who painted knives first. Who painted knives first. Who said who painted knives first. Who said who painted knives first. And see the difference.

INSISTED.

I insisted upon it in summer as well as in winter. I insisted upon it I insisted upon it in summer I insisted upon it in summer as well as in winter. To remember in winter that it is winter and in summer that it is summer. I insisted upon it in summer as well as in winter not sentimentally with raspberries.

TO REMIND.

She reminded me that I was as ready as not and I said I will not say that I preferred service to opposition. I will not say what or what is not a pleasure.

SEVEN.

If she follows let her go, one two three four five six seven. She is let go if she follows. If she follows she is let go. If she follows let her go, she is let go if she follows.

A HAT.

It is as pleasant as that to have a hat, to have a hat and it is as pleasant as that. It is as pleasant as that to have a hat. It is as pleasant as that. To have a hat. To have a hat it is as pleasant as that to have a hat. To have had a hat it is as pleasant as that to have a hat.

HOW TO REMEMBER.

A pretty dress and a pretty hat and how to come, leave out two and how to come. A pretty dress and a pretty hat leave out two. How to come and leave out two. A pretty hat and a pretty dress a pretty dress and a pretty hat and leave out two. Leave out two and and how to come.

A WISH.

And always not when absently enough and heard and said. He had a wish.

FIFTY.

Fifty fifty and fifty-one, she said she thought so and she was told that that was about what it was. Not in place considered as places. Julia was used only as cake, Julia cake was used only as Julia. In some countries cake is called candy. The next is as much as that. When do they is not the same as why do they.

AS A WIFE HAS A COW

A Love Story

Nearly all of it to be as a wife has a cow, a love story. All of it to be as a wife has a cow, all of it to be as a wife has a cow, a love story.

As to be all of it as to be a wife as a wife has a cow, a love story, all of it as to be all of it as a wife all of it as to be as a wife has a cow a love story, all of it as a wife has a cow as a wife has a cow a love story.

Has made, as it has made as it has made, has made has to be as a wife has a cow, a love story. Has made as to be as a wife has a cow a love story. As a wife has a cow, as a wife has a cow a love story. Has to be as a wife has a cow a love story. Has made as to be as a wife has a cow a love story.

When he can, and for that when he can, for that. When he can and for that when he can. For that. When he can. For that when he can. For that. And when he can and for that. Or that, and when he can. For that and when he can.

And to in six and another. And to and in and six and another. And to and in and six and another. And to in six and and to and in and six and another. And to and in and six and another. And to and six and in and another and and to and six and another and and to and in and six and and to and six and in and another.

In came in there, came in there come out of there. In came in come out of there. Come out there in came in there. Come out of there and in and come out of there. Came in there. Come out of there.

Feeling or for it, as feeling or for it, came in or come in, or come out of there or feeling as feeling or feeling as for it.

As a wife has a cow.

Came in and come out.

As a wife has a cow a love story.

As a love story, as a wife has a cow, a love story.

Not and now, now and not, not and now, by and by not and now, as not, as soon as not not and now, now as soon now, now as soon, and now as soon as soon as now. Just as soon just now just now just as soon just as soon as now. Just as soon as now.

And in that, as and in that, in that and and in that, so that, so that and in that, and in that and so that and as for that and as for that and that. In that. In that and and for that as for that and in that. Just as soon and in that. In that as that and just as soon. Just as soon as that.

Even now, now and even now and now and even now. Not as even now, therefor, even now and therefor, therefor and even now and even now and therefor even now. So not to and moreover and even now and therefor and moreover and even now and so and even now and therefor even now.

Do they as they do so. And do they do so.

We feel we feel. We feel or if we feel if we feel or if we feel. We feel or if we feel. As it is made made a day made a day or two made a day, as it is made a day or two, as it is made a day. Made a day. Made a day. Not away a day. By day. As it is made a day.

On the fifteenth of October as they say, said anyway, what is it as they expect, as they expect it or as they expected it, as they expect it and as they expected it, expect it or for it, expected it and it is expected of it. As they say said anyway. What is it as they expect for it, what is it and it is as they expect of it. What is it. What is it the fifteenth of October as they say as they expect or as they expected as they expect for it. What is it as they say the fifteenth of October as they say and as expected of it, the fifteenth of October as they say, what is it as expected of it. What is it and the fifteenth of October as they say and expected of it.

And prepare and prepare so prepare to prepare and prepare to prepare and prepare so as to prepare, so to prepare and prepare to prepare to prepare for and to prepare for it to prepare, to prepare for it, in preparation, as preparation in preparation by preparation. They will be too busy afterwards to prepare. As preparation prepare, to prepare, as to preparation and to prepare. Out there.

Have it as having having it as happening, happening to have it as having, having to have it as happening. Happening and have it as happening and having it happen as happening and having to have it happen as happening, and my wife has a cow as now, my wife having a cow as now, my wife having a cow as now and having a cow as now and having a cow and having a cow now, my wife has a cow and now. My wife has a cow.

1923

VAN OR TWENTY YEARS AFTER

A Second Portrait of Carl Van Vechten

Twenty years after, as much as twenty years after in as much as twenty years after, after twenty years and so on. It is it is it is it is it is.

If it and as if it, if it or as if it, if it is as if it, and it is as if it and as if it. Or as if it. More as if it. As more. As more as if it. And if it. And for and as if it.

If it was to be a prize a surprise if it was to be a surprise to realise, if it was to be if it were to be, was it to be. What was it to be. It was to be what it was. And it was. So it was. As it was. As it is. Is it as it is. It is and as it is and as it is. And so and so as it was.

Keep it in sight alright.

Not to the future but to the fuchsia.

Tied and untied and that is all there is about it. And as tied and as beside, and as beside and tied. Tied and untied and beside and as beside and as untied and as tied and as untied and as beside. As beside as by and as beside. As by as by the day. By their day and as it may, may be they will may be they may. Has it been reestablished as not to weigh. Weigh how. How to weigh. Or weigh. Weight, state, await, state, late state rate state, state await weight state, in state rate at any rate state weight state as stated. In this way as stated. Only as if when the six sat at the table they all looked for those places together. And each one in that direction so as to speak look down and see the same as weight. As weight for weight as state to state as wait to wait as not so. Beside.

For arm absolutely for arm.

They reinstate the act of birth.

Bewildering is a nice word but it is not suitable at present.

They meant to be left as they meant to be left, as they meant to be left left and their center, as they meant to be left and their center. So that in their and do, so that in their and to do. So suddenly and at his request. Get up and give it to him and so suddenly and as his request. Request to request in request, as request, for a request by request, requested, as requested as they requested, or so have it to be nearly there. Why are the three waiting, there are more than three. One two three four five six seven.

As seven.

Seating, regard it as the rapidly increased February.

Seating regard it as the very regard it as their very nearly regard as their very nearly or as the very regard it as the very settled, seating regard it as the very as their very regard it as their very nearly regard it as the very nice, seating regard as their very nearly regard it as the very nice, known and seated, seating regard it, seating and regard it, regard it as the very nearly center left and in the center, regard it as the very left and in the center. And so I say so. So and so. That. For. For that. And for that. So and so and for that. And for that and so and so. And so I say so.

Now to fairly see it have, now to fairly see it have and now to fairly see it have. Have and to have. Now to fairly see it have and to have. Naturally.

As naturally, naturally as, as naturally as. As naturally. Now to fairly see it have as naturally.

Finis

1923

IF I TOLD HIM

A Completed Portrait of Picasso

If I told him would he like it. Would he like it if
I told him.

Would he like it would Napoleon would Napoleon
would would he like it.

If Napoleon if I told him if I told him if Napoleon.
Would he like it if I told him if I told him if Napoleon.
Would he like it if Napoleon if Napoleon if I told him.
If I told him if Napoleon if Napoleon if I told him. If
I told him would he like it would he like it if I told him.

Now.

Not now.

And now.

Now.

Exactly as as kings.

Feeling full for it.

Exactitude as kings.

So to beseech you as full as for it.

Exactly or as kings.

Shutters shut and open so do queens. Shutters shut and shutters and so shutters shut and shutters and so and so shutters and so shutters shut and so shutters shut and shutters and so. And so shutters shut and so and also. And also and so and so and also.

Exact resemblance. To exact resemblance the exact resemblance as exact as a resemblance, exactly as resembling, exactly resembling, exactly in resemblance exactly a resemblance, exactly and resemblance. For this is so. Because.

Now actively repeat at all, now actively repeat at all, now actively repeat at all.

Have hold and hear, actively repeat at all.

I judge judge.

As a resemblance to him.

Who comes first. Napoleon the first.

Who comes too coming coming too, who goes there, as they go they share, who shares all, all is as all as as yet or as yet.

Now to date now to date. Now and now and date and the date.

Who came first Napoleon at first. Who came first Napoleon the first. Who came first, Napoleon first.

Presently.

Exactly do they do.

First exactly.

Exactly do they do too.

First exactly.

And first exactly.

Exactly do they do.

And first exactly and exactly.

And do they do.

At first exactly and first exactly and do they do.

The first exactly.

And do they do.

The first exactly.

At first exactly.

First as exactly.

As first as exactly.

Presently

As presently.

As as presently.

He he he he and he and he and and he and he and he and and as and as he and as he and he. He is and as he is, and as he is and he is, he is and as he and he and as he is and he and he and and he and he.

Can curls rob can curls quote, quotable.

As presently.

As exactitude.

As trains

Has trains.

Has trains.

As trains.

As trains.

Presently.

Proportions.

Presently.

As proportions as presently.

Father and farther.

Was the king or room.

Farther and whether.

Was there was there was there what was there was there what was there was there there was there.

Whether and in there.

As even say so.

One.

I land.

Two.

I land.

Three.

The land.

Three

The land.

Three

The land.

Two

I land.

Two

I land.

One

I land.

Two

I land.

As a so.

They cannot.

A note.

They cannot.

A float.

They cannot

They dote.

IF I TOLD HIM

They cannot.
They as denote.
Miracles play.
Play fairly.
Play fairly well.
A well.
As well.
As or as presently.
Let me recite what history teaches. History teaches.

1923

JEAN COCTEAU

Needs be needs be needs be near.
Needs be needs be needs be.
This is where they have their land astray.
                    Two say.
This is where they have their land astray
Two say.
Needs be needs be needs be
Needs be needs be needs be near.
                    Second time.
It may be nearer than two say.
Near be near be near be
Needs be needs be needs be
Needs be needs be needs be near.
He was a little while away.
Needs be nearer than two say.
Needs be needs be needs be needs be.
Needs be needs be needs be near.
He was away a little while.

And two say.

He was away a little while

He was away a little while

And two say.

Part two

Part two and part one

Part two and part two

Part two and part two

Part two and part one.

He was near to where they have their land astray.

He was near to where they have two say.

Part two and near one. Part one and near one.

Part two and two say.

Part one and part two and two say.

He was as when they had nearly their declamation
their declaration their verification their amplification
their rectification their elevation their safety their share
and there where. This is where they have the land astray.
Two say.

Put it there in there there where they have it. Put it
there in there there where they halve it.

Put it there in there there and they have it. Put it there in there there and they halve it.

He nearly as they see the land astray.

By that and in that and mine.

He nearly as they see he nearly as they see the land he nearly as they see the land astray.

And by that by that time mine. He nearly as they see the land astray by that by that time by that time by that time mine by that time mine by that time. By that time and mine and by that time and mine.

He nearly when they see the land astray.

By that time and mine.

Not nearly apart.

Part and not partly and not apart and not nearly not apart.

When he when he was is and does, when he partly when he partly when he is and was and partly when he and partly when he does and was and is and partly and apart and when he and apart and when he does and was and when he is.

When he is partly

When he is apart.

Particularly for him

He makes it be the rest of the day for them as well.

Partly partly begun

The rest and one

One part partly begun.

Partly begun one and one.

One and one and partly begun and one and one partly begun. Partly begun part partly begun part partly begun and one and part and one and partly begun and part partly begun.

Partly begun.

Did they need the land astray.

Partly begun and one.

Did they need the land astray and partly begun and one.

Did they need it to be the rest of the day did they need it to be the land astray partly begun and one part partly begun part part partly begun part partly begun and one.

They need it as they had it for themselves to be the rest and next to that and by this who were as it must for them.

He knew and this.

When half is May how much is May.

Whole and here there and clear shall and dear well and well at that. Well is a place from which water is drawn and what is drawn.

A well is a place from which out of which water is drawn and what is drawn.

A well is a place out of which water is drawn and water is drawn. A well is a place out of which water is drawn and what is drawn.

A well is a place out of which water is drawn.

A well is a place from which water is drawn.

They made it that they could be where they were.

Where they were when they were where they were.

He had it as is his in his hand.

Hand and head

Head and hand and land

two say

as

ours.

They make them they make them they make them they make them they make them they make them they make them at once.

And nearly when he knows.

As long as head as short as said as short as said as long as head.

And this as long and this as long and this and this and so who makes the wedding go and so and so.

It is usually not my habit to mention anything but now having the habit of addressing I am mentioning it as anything.

Having the habit of addressing having the habit of expressing having the habit of expressing having the habit of addressing.

A little away

And a little way.

Everything away.

Everything away.

Everything and away.

Everything and away.

Away everything away.

It is very extraordinary that it is just as interesting.

When it was it was it was there

There there.

Eight eight and eight, eight eight and eight. Eight eight and eight and and eight.

After all seeing it with that and with that never having heard a third a third too, too.

When there a there and where is where and mine is mine and in is in who needs a shred.

They needed three when this you see when this

you see and three and three and it was two more
they must.

They must address with tenderness
Two him.

G. STEIN

It was not always finished for this once.

Once or twice and for this then they had that and as
well as having it so that and this and all and now and
believe for it all when they and shall and when and for
and most and by and with and this and there and as and
by and will and when and can and this and this and than
and there and find and there and all and with and will
it and with it and with it and they and this and there
and so and I and in and all and all and if and if and if
and if and if and if now. Now need never alter anyhow.

Anyhow means furls furls with a chance chance with
a change change with as strong strong with as will will
with as sign sign with as west west with as most most
with as in in with as by by with as change change with
as reason reason to be lest lest they did when when
they did for for they did there and then. Then does not
celebrate the there and then.

Who knows it.

I wish to be very well pleased and I thank you.

GERTRUDE STEIN.

1925

THE LIFE OF JUAN
GRIS THE LIFE AND
DEATH OF JUAN GRIS

Juan Gris was one of the younger children of a well to do merchant of Madrid. The earliest picture he has of himself is at about five years of age dressed in a little lace dress standing beside his mother who was very sweet and pleasantly maternal looking. When he was about seven years old his father failed in business honorably and the family fell upon very hard times but in one way and another two sons and a daughter lived to grow up well educated and on the whole prosperous. Juan went to the school of engineering at Madrid and when about seventeen came to Paris to study. He tells delightful stories of his father and Spanish ways which strangely enough he never liked. He had very early a very great attraction and love for french culture. French culture has always seduced me he was fond of saying. It seduces me and then I am seduced over again. He used to tell how Spaniards love not to resist temptation. In order to please them the better class merchants such as his father would always have to leave many little things about everything else being packages carefully tied up and in the back on shelves. He used to dwell upon the lack of trust and comradeship in Spanish life. Each one is a general or does not fight and if he does not fight each one is a general. No one that is no Spaniard can help any one because no one no Spaniard can help any one. And this being so and it is so Juan Gris was a brother and comrade to every one being one as no one ever had been one. That is the proportion. One to any one number of millions. That is any proportion. Juan Gris was that one. French culture was always a seduction. Bracque who was such a one was always a seduction seducing french culture seducing again and again. Josette equable intelligent faithful spontaneous delicate courageous delightful forethoughtful, the school of Fontainebleau delicate deliberate measured and free all these things seduced. I am seduced and then I am seduced over again he was fond of saying. He had his own Spanish gift of intimacy. We were intimate. Juan knew what he did. In the beginning he did all sorts of things he used to draw for humorous illustrated papers he had a child a boy named George he lived about he was not young and enthusiastic. The first serious exhibition of his pictures was at the Galerie Kahnweiler rue Vignon in 1914. As a Spaniard he knew cubism and had stepped through into it. He had stepped through it. There was beside this perfection. To have it shown you. Then came the war and desertion. There was little aid. Four years partly illness much perfection and rejoining beauty and perfection and then at the end there came a definite creation of something. This is what is to be measured. He made something that is to be measured. And that is that something.

Therein Juan Gris is not anything but more than anything. He made that thing. He made the thing. He made a thing to be measured.

Later having done it he could be sorry it was not why they liked it. And so he made it very well loving and he made it with plainly playing. And he liked a knife and all but reasonably. This is what is made to be and he then did some stage setting. We liked it but nobody else could see that something is everything. It is everything if it is what is it. Nobody can ask about measuring. Unfortunately. Juan could go on living. No one can say that Henry Kahnweiler can be left out of him. I remember he said "Kahnweiler goes on but no one buys anything and I said it to him and he smiled so gently and said I was everything." This is the history of Juan Gris.

1927

IDENTITY A POEM

I am I because my little dog knows me. The figure wanders on alone.

The little dog does not appear because if it did then there would be nothing to fear.

It is not known that anybody who is anybody is not alone and if alone then how can the dog be there and if the little dog is not there is it alone. The little dog is not alone because no little dog could be alone. If it were alone it would not be there.

So then the play has to be like this.

The person and the dog are there and the dog is there and the person is there and where oh where is their identity, is the identity there anywhere.

I say two dogs but say a dog and a dog.

The human mind.	The human mind does play.
The human mind.	Plays because it plays.
Human nature.	Does not play because it does not play again.

It might desire something but it does not play again.

And so to make excitement and not nervousness into a play.

And then to make a play with just the human mind.

Let us try.

To make a play with human nature and not anything of the human mind.

Pivoines smell like magnolias

Dogs smell like dogs

Men smell like men

And gardens smell differently at different seasons of the year.

PLAY 2

Try a play again.

Every little play helps.

Another play.

There is any difference between resting and waiting.

Does a little dog rest.

Does a little dog wait.

What does the human mind do.

What does human nature do.

A PLAY

There is no in between in a play.

A play could just as well only mean two.

Then it could do

It could really have to do.

The dog.	What could it do.
The human mind.	The human mind too
Human nature.	Human nature does not have it to do.

What can a dog do and with waiting too.

Yes there is when you have been told not to cry.

Nobody knows what the human mind is when they are drunk.

Everybody who has a grandfather has had a great

grandfather and that great grandfather has had a father. This actually is true of a grandmother who was a granddaughter and grandfather had a father.

Any dog too.

Any time any one who knows how to write can write to any brother.

Not a dog too.

A dog does not write too.

ANOTHER PLAY

But. But is a place where they can cease to distress her.

ANOTHER PLAY

It does not make any difference what happens to anybody if it does not make a difference what happens to them.

This no dog can say.

Not any dog can say not ever when he is at play.

And so dogs and human nature have no identity.

It is extraordinary that when you are acquainted with a whole family you can forget about them.

ANOTHER PLAY

A man coming.

Yes there is a great deal of use in a man coming but will he come at all if he does come will he come here.

How do you like it if he comes and looks like that. Not at all later. Well any way he does come and if he likes it he will come again.

Later when another man comes

He does not come.

Girls coming. There is no use in girls coming.

Well any way he does come and if he likes it he will come again.

PART IV
THE QUESTION OF IDENTITY.

A PLAY

I am I because my little dog knows me.

Which is he.

No which is he.

Say it with tears, no which is he.
I am I why.
So there.
I am I where.

ACT I SCENE III

I am I because my little dog knows me.

ACT I SCENE

Now this is the way I had played that play.
But not at all not as one is one.

ACT I SCENE I

Which one is there I am I or another one.

Who is one and one or one is one.

I like a play of acting so and so and a dog my dog is any one of not one.

But we we in America are not displaced by a dog oh no no not at all not at all at all displaced by a dog.

SCENE I

A dog chokes over a ball because it is a ball that choked any one.

PART I SCENE I

He has forgotten that he has been choked by a ball no not forgotten because this one the same one is not the one that can choke any one.

SCENE I ACT I

I am I because my little dog knows me, but perhaps he does not and if he did I would not be I. Oh no oh no.

ACT I SCENE

When a dog is young he seems to be a very intel-ligent one.

But later well later the dog is older.

And so the dog roams around he knows the one he knows but does that make any difference.

A play is exactly like that.

Chorus   There is no left or right without remembering.

And remembering.

They say there is no left and right without remembering.

Chorus   But there is no remembering in the human mind.

Tears   There is no chorus in the human mind.

The land is flat from on high and when they wander.

Chorus   Nobody who has a dog forgets him. They may leave him behind.

Oh yes they may leave him behind.

Chorus   There is no memory in the human mind.

And the result

May be and the result

If I am I then my little dog knows me.

The dog listens while they prepare food.

Food might be connected with the human mind but it is not.

SCENE II

And how do you like what you are

And how are you what you are

And has this to do with the human mind.

Chorus   And has this to do with the human mind.

Chorus   And is human nature not at all interesting.

It is not.

SCENE II

I am I because my little dog knows me.

Chorus   That does not prove anything about you it only proves something about the dog.

Chorus   Of course nobody can be interested in human nature.

Chorus   Nobody is.

Chorus   Nobody is interested in human nature.

Chorus   Not even a dog

Chorus   It has nothing to do human nature has nothing to do with anything.

Chorus   No not with a dog

Tears   No not with a dog.

Chorus   I am I because my little dog knows

Chorus   Yes there I told you human nature is not at all interesting.

SCENE III

And the human mind.

Chorus   And the human mind

Tears   And the human mind

Chorus   Yes and the human mind.

Of course the human mind

Has that anything to do with I am I because my little dog knows me.

What is the chorus.

Chorus   What is the chorus.

Anyway there is the question of identity.

What is the use of being a little boy if you are to grow up to be a man.

Chorus   No the dog is not the chorus.

SCENE II

Any scene may be scene II

Chorus   And act II

No any act can be act one and two.

SCENE II

I am I because my little dog knows me even if the little dog is a big one and yet a little dog knowing me does not really make me be I no not really because after all being I I am I has really nothing to do with the little dog knowing me, he is my audience, but an audience never does prove to you that you are you.

And does a little dog making a noise make the same noise.

He can almost say the b in bow wow.

I have not been mistaken.

Chorus   Some kinds of things not and some kinds of things.

SCENE I

I am I yes sir I am I.

I am I yes madame am I I.

When I am I am I I.

And my little dog is not the same thing as I am I.

Chorus   Oh is it.

With tears in my eyes oh is it.

Yes madame or am I I.

And there we have the whole thing

Am I I.

And if I am I because my little dog knows me am I I.

Yes sir am I I.

The dog answers without asking because the dog is the answer to anything that is that dog.

But not I.

Without tears but not I.

ACT I SCENE I

The necessity of ending is not the necessity of beginning.

Chorus   How finely that is said.

SCENE II

An end of a play is not the end of a day.

SCENE IV

After giving.

1935

WHAT DOES SHE SEE WHEN SHE SHUTS HER EYES

A Novel

It is very meritorious to work very hard in a garden equally so when there is good weather and something grows or when there is very bad weather and nothing grows.

When she shuts her eyes she sees the green things among which she has been working and then as she falls asleep she sees them be a little different. The green things then have black roots and the black roots have red stems and then she is exhausted.

Naturally as she works in the garden she grows strawberries and raspberries and she eats them and sometimes the dog eats them and for days after he is not well and finally he is so weak he cannot stand but in a little while he is ready to eat again.

And so a day is not really a day because each day is like another day and they begin to have nothing. She herself was in mourning because her mother had died, her grandmother was dead before her mother died and her father had curly hair and took off his hat so that his eyes could see that somebody had stopped to talk with him.

It is a pleasure to be afraid of nothing. If they have no children they are not afraid of anything.

A good many of them only have one child and that is not the same as not having any children. If they are married and have no children then they are afraid. But if they are not married and have no child then they are not afraid.

Never having seen him before he becomes your servant and lives in the house and just as intimate as if he had been a father or children. It is funny that, there seems to be so much need of having always known anybody and he comes to answer an advertisement and you never saw him before and there you live in the house with him.

After all nothing changes but the weather and when she shuts her eyes she does not see clouds or sky but she sees woods and green things growing.

So the characters in this novel are the ones who walk

in the fields and lose their dog and the ones who do not walk in the fields because they have no cows.

But everybody likes to know their name. Their name is Gabrielle and Therese and Bertha and Henry Maximilian Arthur and Genevieve and at any time they have happened to be happy.

CHAPTER ONE

How often could they be afraid.

Gabrielle said to any one, I like to say sleep well to each one, and he does like to say it.

He likes to do one thing at a time a long time.

More sky in why why do they not like to have clouds be that color.

Remember anything being atrocious.

And then once in a while it rains. If it rains at the wrong time there is no fruit if it rains at the right time there are no roses. But if it rains at the wrong time then the wild roses last a long time and are dark in color darker than white.

And this makes Henry Maximilian Arthur smile. It is just like the weather to be agreeable because it can be hot enough and so it might just as well not be hot yet. Which it is not.

And therefore Henry Maximilian Arthur is not restless nor is he turned around.

CHAPTER II

She grew sweet peas and carrots and beets. She grew tomatoes and roses and pinks and she grew pumpkins and corn and beans. She did not grow salad or turnips nor camelias nor nasturtiums but nasturtiums do grow and so do hortensias and heliotrope and fuchsias and peonies. After she was very careful she refused to pay more than they were worth and this brings Henry Maximilian Arthur to the contemplation of money. He might even not then throw it away. He might. After all he clings very tightly to what he has. But not to money because about that there is no need. Money is needful those who can move about. And as yet Henry Maximilian Arthur does not do so.

No matter who has left him where he is no matter no matter who has left him where he is no matter. There he is.

No matter. It does not matter that no one has left any one where he is. It does not matter.

All birds look as if they enjoyed themselves and all birds look as if they looked as if they enjoyed themselves.

Better is not different than does it matter. It is better even if it does not matter.

Once in a while Henry Maximilian Arthur was caressed by Theresa. When Theresa caressed Henry Maximilian Arthur Henry Maximilian Arthur liked it as well as he liked it better. That is what is the way in which it was that it did as well as it did not matter.

Grasses grow and they make a shadow so just as grasses grow.

Henry Maximilian Arthur could be tickled by grasses as they grow and he could not caress but he could be caressed by Theresa as well as be tickled by grasses as they grow, when grass is cut it is called hay.

A year of grass is a year of alas. When grass grows that is all that grows but grass is grass and alas is alas.

Once evening morning Henry Maximilian Arthur was awake. Once every morning he was awake and Theresa was not there and when Theresa came Henry Maximilian Arthur was there just the same.

That is what adding means and a cow. Henry Maximilian Arthur had no need of a cow. Theresa did Theresa had need of a cow, but a cow died and that was a loss a loss of a cow and the loss of the value of the cow and to replace the cow there had to be a medium sized cow and a very small cow. But Henry Maximilian Arthur did not share the anxiety.

1936

A WATERFALL
AND A PIANO

There are so many ways in which there is no crime.
A goat comes into this story too.
There is always coincidence in crime.

Helen was an orphan that is to say her mother was put away and her father the major was killed in the war.

He went to the war to be killed in the war because his wife was crazy. She behaved strangely when she went to church. She even behaved strangely when she did not. She played the piano and at the same time put cement between the keys so that they would not sound. You see how easy it is to have cement around.

I have often noticed how easy it is to have cement around. Everywhere there are rocks and so everywhere if you have the necessary building and equipment you have cement.

So the mother was put away and the father was dead and the girl was an orphan.

She went to stay where there was a water-fall. Somewhere there some one had two beautiful dogs that were big. One of them was a male and the other was a female, they were to have puppies, their owner a woman wealthy and careful too always wore carpenter's trousers and carpenter's shirts and loved to work. She said when the puppies came there would be nine and they would need more milk than their mother had. She said this was always so. So she said she would buy a goat.

It is difficult to buy a goat not that goats are really rare, but they are not here and there.

A veterinary who could save lives dogs' lives, cows' lives, sheep's lives and even goats' lives he was not so good about horses, because his father and his grandfather had been veterinaries, even his sister always knew what to do, was asked to find a goat a healthy goat. He found one, the goat had been bought and paid for and then no one would let the goat go. This often happens.

Do you see how the whole place was ready now for anybody to be dead.

With them lived an Englishwoman, this was all in France, and the rest were French.

The more you see how the country is the more you do not wonder why they shut the door. They the women do in a way and yet if they did not it would be best.

There are many places where every one is married even in the country, some of them are not. Think of it even in the country some of them are not.

The Englishwoman was not. She was not married. The French women either had been or were going to be, but the Englishwoman never had been nor was going to be.

She took care of the gardens and chickens and the nine puppies when they came and she did without the goat, and then she went away for a month's holiday and then she came back.

In the meantime well not in the meantime because they had always known each other the orphan stayed with the lady who had the nine puppies.

Nobody refuses fear. Not only for themselves but for their dreams because water as if it were a precipice in the moon-light can not disturb because of there being no origin in their dreams.

The Englishwoman came back. She was very cheerful and had seen all her friends and had plans for the nine puppies and the rest of the garden.

Then the dogs found her. She had put her cap beside her and there were two bullets in her head and she was dead.

The police disturbed her they had no business to, the protestant pastor buried her he had no business to, because nobody had been told what had happened to her.

The doctor said nobody could shoot themselves twice. All the doctors said that. An officer said that this was not so. During the war when an officer wanted to be dead he often put a bullet into his head. But it was very often true, that he did not succeed in doing more than putting a bullet into his scalp and then he sent a second one after.

Anyway she was dead, and her family she had a family in England were not satisfied they were satisfied that she was dead oh yes they were satisfied as to that. And the character of the lady who had the nine puppies she kept them all changed and remained changed ever after. And the orphan married an officer.

And every one still talks about it all but not so much now as they did. An American comes to visit in place of the Englishwoman but she has not come to be dead.

1936

Editor's Note

Stein composed her works by hand, usually writing through the night, in notebooks – some of heavy black oilcloth, others softcover school exercise books with educational pictures on their covers – from which Toklas would type up a clean version for Stein to correct and sometimes revise. In Stein's surviving notebooks, drafts intermingle with shopping lists, doodles, addresses and telephone numbers, and dedications to Toklas. She usually wrote in pencil, scrawling right across the page with just a few words to a line; her texts often end when a notebook is full. Printed versions of Stein's work are, inevitably, stripped of the process that brought them to being; her manuscripts (held in eighty-five boxes at Yale University's Beinecke Library) contain vital clues to the circumstances of each text's composition, but also invite complex textual questions.

A comparison of manuscript, typescript and printed text reveals intriguing discrepancies that are difficult to resolve: individual words, punctuation marks or line spacings sometimes differ, and on rare occasions entire phrases or sentences have been transposed, added, or deleted. 'Identity a Play' became 'Identity a Poem; 'Alice' became 'Ada'; passages marked 'Y. D.' – Stein's customary sign-off in private love notes to Toklas – have been silently incorporated into the main text.

Where published editions differ from typescripts, and typescripts from manuscripts, it's impossible to be certain whether anomalies represent mistakes on the part of Toklas (Stein's handwriting was notoriously difficult to read), printer's errors, or edits authorised by Stein herself. In preparing this edition, I have followed the authoritative texts printed in *A Stein Reader* (Northwestern University Press, 1993), edited by Ulla Dydo; for texts not in that book, I have followed the first editions, with a few very minor emendations where I judged that discrepancies represented transcription errors rather than corrections. Stein rarely used accents on French words; her capitalisation was unsystematic, and she didn't particularly value consistency in spelling: all these idiosyncrasies have been preserved.

FIRST PLACES OF PUBLICATION

Ada
Geography and Plays (Boston: Four Seas Company, 1922)

Matisse
Camera Work, August 1912

Picasso
Camera Work, August 1912

Miss Furr and Miss Skeene
Geography and Plays (Boston: Four Seas Company, 1922)

Flirting at the Bon Marche
Two: Gertrude Stein and Her Brother, and Other Early Portraits (1908-12)
    (New Haven: Yale University Press, 1951)

Portrait of Mabel Dodge at the Villa Curonia
privately printed, 1912; *Camera Work*, June 1913

Susie Asado
Geography and Plays (Boston: Four Seas Company, 1922)

Preciosilla
Composition as Explanation (London: Hogarth Press, 1926)

What Happened: A Five Act Play
Geography and Plays (Boston: Four Seas Company, 1922)

Sacred Emily
Geography and Plays (Boston: Four Seas Company, 1922)

One: Carl Van Vechten
Geography and Plays (Boston: Four Seas Company, 1922)

Advertisements
Geography and Plays (Boston: Four Seas Company, 1922)

Ladies' Voices: Curtain Raiser
Geography and Plays (Boston: Four Seas Company, 1922)

Accents in Alcace
Geography and Plays (Boston: Four Seas Company, 1922)

A Movie
Operas and Plays (Paris: Plain Edition, 1932)

A Saint in Seven
Composition as Explanation (London: Hogarth Press, 1926)

Idem the Same: A Valentine to Sherwood Anderson
Little Review 9, spring 1923

Cezanne
Portraits and Prayers (New York: Random House, 1934)

A Book Concluding with As A Wife Has a Cow A Love Story
(Paris: Editions de la Galerie Simon, 1926)

Van or Twenty Years After: A Second Portrait of Carl Van
   Vechten
Portraits and Prayers (New York: Random House, 1934)

If I Told Him: A Completed Portrait of Picasso
Vanity Fair 21 no 8, April 1924

Jean Cocteau
Composition as Explanation (London: Hogarth Press, 1926)

The Life of Juan Gris The Life and Death of Juan Gris
transition no 4, July 1927

Identity a Poem
What Are Masterpieces? (California: Conference Press, 1940)

What Does She See When She Shuts Her Eyes
Mrs Reynolds and Five Earlier Novelettes (New Haven: Yale University
   Press, 1952)

A Waterfall and a Piano
New Directions in Prose and Poetry (Norfolk: New Directions, 1936)